THE ACCIDENT REPORT

a RONALD TRULUCK novel

RALPH ELLIS

Black Rose Writing | Texas

ISBN: 978-1-68513-617-8
LIBRARY OF CONGRESS CONTROL NUMBER: 2025933035
PUBLISHED BY BLACK ROSE WRITING
www.blackrosewriting.com

Printed in the United States of America
Suggested Retail Price (SRP) $19.95

The Accident Report is printed in Garamond Premier Pro

*As a planet-friendly publisher, Black Rose Writing does its best to eliminate unnecessary waste to reduce paper usage and energy costs, while never compromising the reading experience. As a result, the final word count vs. page count may not meet common expectations.

Cover design by Paolo Aguila

For Susan Puckett

PRAISE FOR
THE ACCIDENT REPORT

"Ralph Ellis delights the reader with engaging characters, a suspenseful plot, and laugh-out-loud humor."
–Kim McCollum, author of *What Happens in Montana*

"*The Accident Report* is a reminder of the importance of local journalism and a throwback to the days when the field was thriving. It's an enjoyable read that had me nodding along in delight with each new twist or character introduction."
–Philip Reari, author of *Earth Jumped Back*

"Solid and fully formed characters, off-beat dialogue, and a twisty plot carry the story along very nicely. The fondly detailed nostalgia about a world that no longer exists only adds to this satisfying and entertaining novel."
–Gojan Nikolich, author of *The Gopher King: A Dark Comedy*, *Tiger Season: A Novel of Korea*, and *Ashes in Venice: A Vengeance Thriller*

"Ellis's descriptions of 1970s-era scenarios and capers, and his droll commentary on Truluck's haphazard investigations, were so laugh-inducing I stopped reading periodically—to quote entire sections to my husband."
–Jann Alexander, author of *Unspoken: A Dust Novel*

"Ralph Ellis delivers this solid narrative with a great pace and a tongue in cheek attitude. ... A refreshing approach and one that is entertaining and works."
–Paul Jantzen, author of *Sour Apples*

"The small-town south is its own thing, and Ralph Ellis captures it perfectly. Mountains out of molehills, molehills out of mountains, quirky characters, fabulous '70s atmosphere. ... Ellis is a talented writer with pitch-perfect dialogue and insight into what makes communities tick."
–Lori B. Duff, author of *Devil's Defense* and *Devils Hand*, Fisher at Law Novels

"*The Accident Report* is a loving tribute to old-school, shoe-leather reporting and establishes Ralph Ellis as a first-rate satirist."
–*Queen City Nerve*, Charlotte's alternative newspaper

"*The Accident Report* is an entertaining mystery with plenty of laughs."
–Mickey Dubrow, author of *The Magic Maker, Bulletproof,* and *American Judas*

"Ronald Truluck's mix of courage and bumbling missteps makes him a compelling, deeply human protagonist you'll want to hug, or give a swift kick in the behind."
–Ronald Aiken, author of *Death Has Its Benefits*

THE ACCIDENT REPORT

CHAPTER ONE

On the day Richard Nixon resigned the presidency, Ronald Truluck drove the long way to work so he could smoke a celebratory joint. He was a reporter, a member of the profession that uncovered Nixon's misdeeds and saved the republic. But Ronald had never written about Watergate. His paper, *The Eagle,* only reported the news of Millerton, North Carolina, and did so in microscopic detail. Pet-of-the-week pictures on the front page. New garden club officers. And car wreck stories, Ronald's responsibility as police reporter. *The Eagle* was a long way from *The Washington Post*, but Ronald felt like he had landed on the right side of history.

He accelerated onto the Millerton bypass and fired up his last joint of Colombian redbud. He'd been saving it for a special occasion, such as the president resigning or the release of a new Rolling Stones album. The wind whipped his shoulder-length hair. He clicked on the AM radio. The guitar solo on the Allman Brothers' "Ramblin' Man" rang out of the little speakers. He was riding a happy buzz when he parked his car at the newspaper and set out on foot to cover the police beat. He crossed an asphalt parking lot to Millerton City Hall, where trustees wearing black-and-white jumpsuits tended the lawn. An armed deputy watched to make sure nobody escaped. That was an overexertion of police authority, but Ronald waved to the deputy, like it didn't bother him. Since graduating from college and taking the job, he made ethical compromises on an hourly basis.

The police station was in the city hall basement with an entrance around back. Ronald pushed open double doors and stepped into a tiny lobby. It smelled of sweat, desperation, and insecticide. He visited this place at least once a day, five days a week. The lobby didn't have chairs or even a bench because the police didn't want people hanging around for no reason. The dome light below the slow-moving ceiling fan held seven or eight dead bugs. He drummed his fingers on the wooden counter to announce himself. Betty Stokes, the desk sergeant, rocked out of a chair, hitched up her police pants, and waddled to her side of the counter. She had shaggy hair and wore a too-tight cop uniform with a revolver in a holster.

"Need to see the stuff," Ronald said.

Betty handed him a clipboard holding a sheaf of police reports. A two-foot-long chain attached the clipboard to the counter so nobody would steal it. "You're welcome," she said and laid her freckled forearm on the counter like she didn't have anything to do besides watch him work. Betty's breath smelled like swamp gas but Ronald didn't turn his head. He needed to stay on her good side because Betty—not the laws approved by the state legislature—controlled his access to the clipboard.

Betty demonstrated her power three weeks earlier after Ronald explained her uncle had died of prostate cancer, not *prostrate* cancer. In retaliation for correcting her, she didn't put an important accident report on the clipboard—a double fatal on the bypass, a big story in Millerton— but made sure it got to Dawn Mourning from Channel 5. Ronald's editors sat him down and explained that getting beat by a larger newspaper in their own backyard was embarrassing, but getting beat by TV was a humiliation. TV was entertainment, not journalism. The unspoken message: Ronald needed to eat a teeny bit of Betty's shit.

He began transcribing information. Law enforcement officers had a habit of violating the laws of grammar. "The Honder 305cc Super Hawk motercicle where stolen from a bakyard shed it were chained," said the report. The handwriting was so bad Betty had to translate. Next came a riding lawn mower theft in which the thief drove it down the street and a misdemeanor marijuana arrest in the parking lot at Exiles on Main Street, the longhair bar.

"Heard something about a wreck on Archdale Street," Betty said, almost whispering, "but don't tell anybody you heard it from me. Okay, Scoop?"

"Of course." Betty had never steered him to a story. Maybe they were on better terms than he thought. "I don't see it on the clipboard."

"It's not on the clipboard. It's somewhere else."

"Like where?"

She shrugged, shook her head, and lifted her palms—a trifecta of ignorance. Why was she lying? Betty knew where every piece of paper in the police department was kept.

"I'm told a car ran into a yard," she offered.

"Anybody hurt?" Personal injury was one of *The Eagle*'s standards for a wreck being newsworthy.

"Nope. Maybe fifty dollars damage to the yard because of the birdbath, and a couple hundred for the car that ran into the birdbath. Heard it was a Bonneville."

"Any unusual circumstances?" The umbrella term for juicy details.

"In my opinion, pretty damn unusual."

"Stick had a wreck?" The rail-thin mayor, Bob Holloway, also known as Stick, was a political lightweight who owned a vacuum cleaner store. *The Eagle* delighted in documenting his idiotic statements. "Or Hawk?" Meaning Miller County Sheriff Dennis Hawkins, with whom the police had a low-level rivalry. "Somebody on the city council?" he asked.

"I better not say anything else."

That was almost a yes, but he was learning Betty's code. He was thinking up a question when a man's voice boomed, "Hello there, Ronald!"

Police Chief Jim Smithers had snuck up behind him. Smithers was an executive cop. Instead of a police uniform, he wore a gray business suit, shiny black wing tips, and black-rimmed glasses. He combed his silver hair straight back. He was as big as an offensive lineman on a college football team and delivered a bone-crusher handshake. Cops always reminded you they had the size and strength advantage.

"Follow me," the chief said and led Ronald through a lobby side door, down a corridor and into his office. It was a carpeted room with leather chairs and hunting prints. Behind a wide desk sat a chunk of a woman in her mid-forties with short gray hair. Ellen Swicegood, the chief's secretary, looked at Ronald like he planned to steal her stapler.

"Where's that press release?" the chief asked. Ellen pulled a sheet of paper from underneath a Bible. "The problem, Ronald," the chief continued, "is people drive too fast in front of the elementary school and we want them to slow down or else we'll have to issue tickets. Could you run this in *The Eagle* for us?"

Ronald said yes. The chief crushed his hand again. Ronald asked what the chief thought about Nixon's resignation. To get his hands on a Watergate story and still abide by *The Eagle*'s focus on local news, Ronald would write a reaction story. He'd telephone the town big shots—like the smug plutocrats who ran the textile mills and a couple of big preachers who didn't handle snakes, as far as anybody knew—to ask what they thought about Watergate wrapping up this way.

"Watergate was a third-rate burglary," the chief said. "What's the big deal?"

"I'm not talking about the break-in at the Democratic national headquarters in the Watergate building," Ronald explained. "I'm talking about Watergate in the larger sense. I mean all the crimes Nixon committed and the corrupt spirit that permeated his administration."

"I know you people in the news media are happy about it, but I'm not," Chief Smithers said. "He hasn't been convicted of a crime. He's been a good president. He shouldn't resign."

Ronald hadn't gotten used to being around so many Nixon defenders. He'd come from the state's flagship university at Chapel Hill where George McGovern, a Democrat, was the consensus choice in the 1972 presidential election. That McGovern lost in a landslide meant the majority of the voters were lacking in education, not that college students were out of touch with the mainstream. He wrote the chief's words in his notebook.

"Also," Ronald said, "I heard something about a wreck on Archdale Street, but the accident report isn't on the clipboard. Can you give me any details?"

"Who told you that?"

"I can't say." Ronald had promised anonymity to Betty without thinking. "Surely you understand about confidential sources. Your own detectives use them."

"We're law enforcement officers. We have the legal right. You're just a reporter."

"I have the legal right," Ronald said, putting himself in the company of Bob Woodward and Carl Bernstein, *The Washington Post* reporters who broke Watergate. He squared his chin, ready to argue.

The barometric pressure in the room dropped. Chief Smithers pulled himself to attention, froze his facial features, and delivered the cop stare. That's the paralyzing, soul-piercing gaze every police officer had mastered when they graduated from the police academy. It establishes the power differential and makes people confess to crimes they haven't committed. It made Ronald feel like a pretender for trying to use unnamed sources. Did the chief intuit he'd smoked a joint that morning? The waterworks opened in his armpits.

"Are you sure an accident happened?" Chief Smithers said. "If your so-called source won't allow their name to be used, there's something fishy going on."

"Liars spread lies to destroy good people," Ellen said.

She almost called Ronald a liar—fighting words. But he couldn't fight a woman, especially Ellen. She'd leave him bleeding on the carpet and send him the cleaning bill. Chief Smithers laid his hand on Ronald's shoulder and guided him into the corridor.

"At this point, no such accident report is available to the press or the public."

"I'm just asking questions," Ronald said. The door shut in his face.

Ronald tingled with a new sensation. For the first time in his career, he had a real story.

CHAPTER TWO

Ronald next checked the reports at the Miller County Sheriff's Department and Millerton Fire Department, his other stops on the police beat, then drove toward Archdale Street to investigate the mysterious wreck. Millerton was well-named. It was a mill town for textiles and furniture. At the hulking Millerton Blanket Factory No. 2, hangdog workers streamed in and out for the shift change. Everybody looked tired, even the people starting their shifts. He cruised down Main Street, which was quaint and ghostlike at the same time. Half the stores had closed since the Kmart shopping center opened on the bypass. That left old-time favorites like the locally owned shoe store and vanity shops catering to Millerton's minuscule upper class, like the Quilt Emporium. Somebody had taped a going-out-of-business sign to the Millerton Hardware window.

He got stuck at the railroad crossing in the middle of town and watched the railcars coast by like wasted moments of his life. What was he doing in Millerton? It was hot and unsightly. He hadn't made any friends. The local girls weren't impressed by his college degree. And his job—he worked for a paper named after a bird that was going extinct. Why hadn't he studied harder in college? Why didn't he apply for summer internships or at least work on the student paper? Then he would have ended up at a real newspaper. He'd been working for *The Eagle* six weeks—half of his three-month probation period—and had nothing to show except dozens of cop briefs and twenty-two byline stories about housefires, car wrecks, and one drunken killing. Nothing to change the arc of American democracy.

He'd tried to show initiative. He saw an incident report about a man, Crosby Melton, who was bitten so badly by his own dog, a German Shepherd named Banjo, that twenty-two stitches were required to close the wounds. That sounded like a human interest story, for man's best friend to turn on his owner. Ronald drove to Crosby's house next to the fertilizer plant. When Crosby opened his front door, Banjo ran onto the porch and bit Ronald on the left shin. The man pulled the dog back inside and yelled through the screen door, "He's had all his shots."

Ronald drove himself to the emergency room, but he didn't need stitches, just a bandage. His editors were amused and made him write a first-person account of what happened. The headline said, "Reporter Sings the Blues After Being Bitten by Dog Named Banjo." Ronald explained a banjo is primarily an instrument used in country and bluegrass, not the blues, but the headline stayed.

He replayed his conversation with Chief Smithers. The chief had chosen his words with care. He didn't deny a wreck happened on Archdale Street, just said an accident report wasn't available. He didn't lie, but he withheld information. It was, in the words of Woodward and Bernstein, a non-denial denial. Like the time Ronald asked his college roommate if he drank the last beer in the refrigerator and his roomie said, "I drank a Coke." The caboose passed, the mechanical arms of the rail crossing lifted, and Ronald hastened to the crime scene.

Archdale Street was lined with ranch houses and cinder-block duplexes on quarter-acre lots. The houses had carports, not garages, and the street had ditches, not sidewalks. Dogs and little boys ran loose. Ronald parked and knocked on doors. At the fourth house, a shirtless man with a spray of freckles across his chest answered.

"Somebody told me a wreck happened around here about a week ago," Ronald said. "That a Bonneville ran into a yard and knocked down a birdbath."

"Heard that too. Didn't see it, though."

"Do you know where it happened?" The man nodded. "Where?" He pointed with his head. "Next door?" Shook his head. "Two doors down?" Shook his head again. Ronald asked him to point out the spot.

"Down the road about a mile, where that ugly yellow car is parked. Can't believe a man would drive a piece of shit like that."

The car snobbery in Millerton was intense. Ronald hitchhiked through college so he didn't have a car when he got hired. Wanting to be helpful, his dad presented him with a graduation gift: a 1966 Ford Galaxie 500. It was a beige car with square corners. It had a bench seat covered in itchy upholstery, a gear shift on the column, and an AM radio that worked most of the time. Ronald said thanks since he was broke and needed a car for the job, but the Galaxie had the personality of a shoe box. The papers in the glove box said it used to be owned by the state department of transportation. For Ronald to drive such a car was an ironic statement, like a hippie wearing an old army jacket, or a peace symbol on a nuclear warhead. So far, nobody got the joke.

He drove down the street which turned from asphalt to dirt as the houses thinned out. A white, frame house at 304 Archdale Street stood alone in a gentle curve, surrounded on three sides by woods. The yellow car parked in the gravel driveway was a Chevy Vega, one of the most reviled subcompacts in America. Their engines ran so hot Vega owners had to carry cases of motor oil in their trunk and add a quart every couple of days. Tire tracks crisscrossed the front yard, indicating a wreck happened not too long ago. In the middle of the grass, smooth river rocks were arranged in a circle three feet in diameter—the perfect spot for a replacement birdbath. This was the place.

Nobody answered at the front door. He walked around to the back and found a man and woman working in a small vegetable garden. Actually, the woman did all the work, chopping the dirt with a hoe while the man stood on the grass and talked. She was in her fifties, wearing a baggy T-shirt, blue jeans with rolled-up cuffs, and tennis shoes without laces. Ronald called out hello and launched into weather talk, not wanting to spook the simple Millerton folk. The woman said, "I know it's hot. I'm sweating like a dog. Who are you?" She had the tired eyes of somebody who'd been screwed over her entire life.

"I'm following a tip from a source who I can't identify, so don't ask me who she is. I won't tell you. I'll go to jail before I tell you or anybody else. I gave her my word."

"What do you mean by 'source'?" the woman said.

"It means somebody who told me something very important. My source said a wreck happened on Archdale Street, though she didn't give me many details, and a second source who I also can't identify"—Ronald forgot to ask the neighbor's name—"said the wreck happened in your yard, that a Bonneville knocked down your birdbath. Is that what happened?"

"We don't want to answer any of your questions," she said. "I can tell you're not with the police department, not with that hair."

Ronald's hair was a wavy bundle of split ends that fell to his shoulders. It was his statement, his freak flag, but he compromised the rest of his look so he could function in Millerton society. He wore a blue oxford shirt with the sleeves rolled up to his elbows, jeans, and penny loafers he loathed. His Converse All-Star sneakers were too casual for the office and cowboy boots hurt his ankles, so he had to wear the shoes his mother bought him for Christmas. They were almost FBI shoes, the phrase Tom Wolfe used in *The Electric Kool-Aid Acid Test* to describe no-personality footwear favored by cops. Ronald would go shoe shopping soon.

"I forgot to identify myself. I'm Ronald Truluck with *The Eagle*."

"*The Eagle*!" the man said. "I read it all the time. I've seen your name on crime stories. You're a very good writer. I'm Bill Jorgensen."

Bill Jorgensen had an intelligent face, not much hair, and gray eyes. He was younger than the woman and wearing office clothes, down to lace-up shoes. His handshake was cool and limp.

"We're not saying if something happened or didn't happen," the woman said while glaring at her husband.

"Sarah, he's just doing his job. There's no need to be hostile to Mr. Truluck."

Mister. One of Ronald's English professors called him Mister and said it with such sarcasm Ronald quit the class. But Jorgensen wasn't being sarcastic. He was sucking up—a new experience for Ronald.

"You can talk," Ronald said. "You have freedom of speech, you know. All citizens do. It's guaranteed in the Bill of Rights. It's the very first amendment because it's the most important." You could never go overboard defending freedom of speech.

"Nothing's free in this world," Sarah said. "You pay for everything one way or the other. Now, I'm telling you for the last time it's none of your business what happened in our yard."

"It's the public's business, and as a journalist, I represent the public. I represent the taxpayers, the citizens of Millerton, the People with a capital P. The person that had a wreck in your yard is a public figure. Who was it?"

Sarah said, "I used a sharpening stone to put an edge on this hoe an hour ago. If you don't move off my property, I'm going to whack your toes off, just like I cut the head off that copperhead last week." She raised the hoe and made chopping motions. Ronald stepped back.

"We'll just say 'no comment' for the moment, if you don't mind," Bill said, and walked him out of the backyard. When they reached the driveway Bill said, "Sorry about my wife. She has a good heart but she's intimidated by literate people."

"Who was the driver? What's with the secrecy?"

Jorgensen moved his mouth, like he was about to say something. "Someday, maybe I'll be able to explain," he said. "In the meantime, there's something else I wanted to ask, though."

"Bill!" the woman yelled, and her husband flinched. She rushed toward them, hoe-less but red-faced. "We're not talking to the reporter."

"I'm not telling him anything about the wreck, Sarah."

"So, it did happen!" Ronald said.

"You and me are going inside and have a come-to-Jesus meeting." She grabbed the inside of her husband's elbow and steered him up the front steps and inside the house, slamming the front door with force. Their moves were choreographed, like they'd done it before.

Seeing the couple interact reinforced Ronald's opinion that marriage was a sham, a piece of paper, a meaningless institution. When you're tied down to somebody, you become the bully or the bullied. How did Bill and Sarah Jorgensen get together? What did Bill want to talk about, if not the wreck? Ronald tore a page out of his reporter's notebook, wrote down his name and phone number, and slid it under the windshield wiper of the Vega. He'd get business cards when his probation period ended.

CHAPTER THREE

The Eagle operated out of a two-story building constructed of fading Depression-era brick one block from city hall, with the newsroom on top, advertising downstairs, and the printing press in a separate building next door. Ronald never set foot in advertising because he held their guiding principle—the pursuit of money, not truth—in contempt.

The newsroom was spartan. It had eight army surplus desks, manual typewriters, black rotary phones, tan carpet, and fake wood paneling. The walls were decorated with a free-for-all of personal photos, newspaper clippings, and farm equipment calendars attached with tape and thumbtacks. A layer of cigarette and pipe smoke hovered at ceiling level. Nobody had a private office. Everybody saw and heard everything that happened.

Ronald dropped into the chair next to editor I.J. Carlton's desk. That's where readers sat when they asked him to run a story about their grandson making the dean's list. Mr. Carlton occupied the best spot in the newsroom, in front of the largest window overlooking the parking lot and beyond it, city hall. State press association awards in black frames hung on the walls beside the windows. He stopped marking up letters to the editor, laid down the No. 2 pencil and turned his long, sad face to Ronald. He dressed like a clerk in a white, short-sleeved, polyester dress shirt with double breast pockets and a black tie—the establishment uniform of every adult man in Ronald's universe. Also, a black eyepatch, like a James Bond villain, though the boldest thing Mr. Carlton had done was change the name of the paper—from *The Millerton Eagle* to *The Eagle*—in an attempt to gain countywide readership.

"I got a comment from Chief Smithers about Nixon," Ronald said. "I could call some other people and put together a Watergate reaction story."

"Write up his comments and give them to Shelly. She came up with the same idea and is already working on it."

Shelly Symington-Haskins, the government reporter, clamped the phone between her ear and shoulder while scribbling notes. This was her first week on the job.

"I came across a big story, an important story," Ronald said and recounted his information about the wreck and his suspicions about the cover-up. He left out Betty Stokes' name. "I'm sure it's somebody on the city council, but nobody will tell me who. Bill Jorgensen wants to tell me something, but his wife made him shut up."

Martha Steadman walked over and joined the conversation. She was a part-time copy editor but had assumed the authority of a full-time second-in-command by just being there all the time. She was hired to work five days a week from two until seven, but she arrived at noon and never left before eleven. Also, she lived with her mother and didn't want to go home.

"Bill Jorgensen is a total nut," Martha said. "I don't like the man. A couple of years ago he showed up at a city council meeting to complain about library funding and ended up saying some pie-in-the-sky things. Like the city should fire firefighters and use the money to buy more books. And he said they should build a subway to reduce dependence on foreign oil. I mean, crazy stuff. Then he called and said we misquoted him. But the reporter had the words in her notebook. I called somebody at city hall who said we got it right. We told Bill no way. Then he comes into the office to complain some more. He called me a liar and a dishonest journalist. I chased him out of the office."

"Then he did that book," Mr. Carlton said, chuckling.

"Oh yeah," Martha said, rolling up the sleeves on her cardigan. "Bill wrote a book of poetry and sent me a press release he wrote. It even had a Polaroid picture of himself. We weren't going to run anything about his book, not after the way he acted. But he called me and wondered if we lost the press release. He talked like we've been good friends for years. I told him to jump in the lake and slammed the phone down. I don't want to see anything in the paper about Bill Jorgensen except his obituary."

"He wants to tell me something," Ronald repeated.

"Don't waste your time," Martha said. "He's a loon. He can't hold a job. I know you want an eyewitness to the wreck, but not Bill Jorgensen."

That made two women who didn't want Bill Jorgensen to talk, his wife and Martha. How could this wimp inspire such a powerful reaction in women? Ronald didn't want to cross Martha. Maybe he'd leave Jorgensen alone, at least for a while.

"Anyway," Ronald said, "I'll need to skip covering the routine police beat stuff next week so I can concentrate on finding out who the driver was. We can't let this kind of corruption go unquestioned."

Nobody echoed his cry for justice. Mr. Carlton said, "Lamont Moody had the wreck. Somebody told me that at the coffee shop."

"You'd already heard about it?" Ronald said. "Why didn't you tell me?"

"I hadn't gotten around to it."

Lewis Daisy, the paper's gaunt and goateed photographer, rushed up. "Lamont was drunk and ran off the road in front of the Jorgensen house, plowed into the birdbath, got out of his car, and made a fool of himself cussing out Sarah. Then a cop took him home."

"Who's your source?" Ronald said. "I need to talk with them."

Lewis removed his hat and ran his fingers through his long hair. After Mr. Carlton, he was the oldest person in the newsroom. "Somebody who'd know. That's all I can say."

Lewis's information was solid. He was in good with the cops. When a bad wreck happened, he developed two sets of black-and-white prints. One was suitable for publication in a family newspaper and the other showed mutilated bodies, which he handed over to the officers for their personal collections. In return, the cops told Lewis the good stuff, bits of which filtered down to Ronald. Mr. Carlton let Lewis walk away without divulging his source. This was a frustrating fact of life at *The Eagle*. Knowing the dirt was more important than printing it.

Ronald said, "Who is Lamont Moody? I know he's on the city council but what else?"

"He owns a heavy equipment company on the bypass," Mr. Carlton said. "Doesn't say much at meetings, so he doesn't look as dumb as the rest of them. He's a jerk."

"You want me to go after this hard, don't you? We've got to bring this guy down."

Mr. Carlton and Martha exchanged a look.

"Before you turn into an investigative reporter, you've got to stop making silly mistakes," Mr. Carlton said. "You know the cop brief you wrote about the man charged with simple possession of marijuana. That was wrong. He really was charged with improper passing. He showed me the ticket when he came in to complain. When the deputy wrote the ticket, he abbreviated the charge as 'imp. pass.' You must have misinterpreted the words as 'simp. poss.' when you saw the ticket at the sheriff's department. Pretty big mistake. The man is a deacon in a church out in the country and says he's never touched drugs or alcohol in his life."

It was Ronald's second error and his biggest. In his other mistake, he wrote that a man shot his brother when it was his half-brother. The police report specified that, but Ronald figured a half-brother was still a brother. Mr. Carlton thought it made a difference.

Mr. Carlton circled the error with a black pencil, opened a desk drawer, and dropped the newspaper page into a folder. Probably marked as "Ronald's screwups." His permanent record. If Ronald was fired for incompetence from a little league paper like *The Eagle*, it would be maximum humiliation. He'd have to change his name and leave the country. He couldn't have felt worse—until Linda Lasseter, his office archenemy, chimed in.

"That man is a good Christian," she said. The highest possible praise. She went back to regurgitating propaganda from the chamber of commerce into a business brief. She didn't respect Ronald, but she should have. He was a reporter while she was only the administrative assistant. She'd buttoned her white blouse tight at the neck and sat ramrod straight, the better to accommodate the stick up her ass.

"I'm not telling you to not ask questions about this so-called wreck, but before you write anything, I need to see the accident report and I need some on-the-record statements," Mr. Carlton said. He touched his eyepatch, one of his nervous tics.

"The police say there's no accident report for me to look at. It's 'under investigation.' Nobody's going to talk unless I promise not to use their name, like in Watergate."

Bringing up Watergate was unavoidable, but it didn't help Ronald's case. Mr. Carlton disliked Nixon—he was "a creep"—but he detested how *The Washington Post* used unnamed sources to break the story. If a reporter couldn't get sources to talk to him on the record, the reporter wasn't working hard enough. Mr. Carlton was a quiet man, but one day he read something about "Deep Throat," Woodward and Bernstein's unnamed informant, and started ranting to the newsroom at large. "It's cheating," he said.

"I figured a young reporter would want to pull something like that," Mr. Carlton said. "You've got to produce some sort of document before we even consider going with that story. I repeat, don't even try to use an anonymous source. We've never used one before. In fact, I'd like eye witnesses. This story involves an elected official, so we need to go the extra mile. And don't try to ignore your daily duties."

Mr. Carlton turned away and started packing his pipe again, a signal he was tired of talking. Ronald got the message. Mr. Carlton was nervous about investigating city hall, but he'd never come out and say so. He had to *look* like a tough editor. He thought Ronald couldn't bring in the story. Ronald would cover his beat and dig into the wreck at the same time. He just had to avoid screwing up again.

Ronald went to his desk. It was old and scuffed, but it was his first desk on his first job, and he was proud of it. He lit a Marlboro with a lighter built into a Budweiser can, then rested the cigarette on an ashtray shaped like a black rubber tire. Copies of *The Eagle, The New York Times, The Washington Post, Rolling Stone,* and *The Winston-Salem Guardian* were stacked along the edge of the desk, creating a low privacy wall. He used to have a framed photo of Che Guevara that Ronald had autographed with the words, "Ronald, you're my greatest inspiration." He put it away because people kept asking if he really knew Fidel Castro's revolutionary comrade.

Ronald started the cop briefs. He wrote: "Leonard Denny can keep on truckin'. His 1966 Ford pickup truck, which was reported stolen at 8:47 a.m. Wednesday from the 32-year-old man's home at 436 Adair St. in Millerton, was located 14 hours later on McKenney Road and returned to him undamaged, Millerton police reported."

He decided not to turn in that brief. Millerton readers would miss the reference to "Truckin'," the Grateful Dead song. He'd start listening to country music, which had many truck-driving references.

He ran out of brain-stimulating cigarettes. He looked in his desk drawer. It contained two yo-yos, a folding knife, restaurant matchbooks, baseball cards, and a pack of playing cards. In the back, a *Penthouse* magazine with a centerfold of a woman who, by rumor, once attended his college. But no cigarettes. Who could he bum a smoke from? Shelly smoked Virginia Slims, which was a woman's cigarette. If Ronald lit up one of those, his sexuality would be questioned. Linda Lasseter and Anne Richmond, the fragrant editor of the women's page, didn't smoke. Lewis the photographer was too intimidating to ask and Mr. Carlton smoked a pipe. That left Snap Tolbert, the sports editor, who was somewhere else talking to a football coach. He searched Snap's drawer, found an opened pack of Winstons, and took two. He finished the other cop briefs and laid them on Martha's desk at the moment Shelly approached.

"Have you read my city council story?" Shelly asked Martha.

"It's fine except in the first reference you neglected to identify Danny Tarlton as the city manager," Martha said. "But I fixed it."

Mild criticism, but Shelly took it hard. She walked slump-shouldered back to her desk, picked up one of her snowglobes and gazed into it.

Martha gestured to the chair beside her desk and Ronald sat. She was around forty with glinting blue eyes and gray teeth from years of drinking newsroom coffee. No wedding ring. She grew up in Millerton and said she knew everybody, including the crooks. She adjusted her glasses and said, "The police say a man shoplifted a bottle of Mad Dog 20/20 from Brandon's Superette. 'Mad Dog' is slang. The actual brand of wine is Mogen David."

She made corrections with a pencil and dropped the brief into a basket labeled "Ready." The brief about the motorcycle theft and the pot arrest were okay. Last, she read the brief about stolen garden tools. She swiveled to her typewriter and typed a headline on a separate piece of paper, attached it with a paperclip to the cop brief, and tossed it into the ready basket.

"These are fine," she said. "Just so you know, Glendon Harris used to be the mayor. He's filed half a dozen theft reports in the last year. He keeps telling the cops somebody's stealing his garden tools and stuff like golf clubs, golf shoes, bags of fertilizer."

"Who's doing it?"

"A lot of people think it's his stepson, Elliott. He's always been kind of messed up. Barely graduated from high school, lives at home and can't hold a job. He never got along with Glendon, who has a temper. Elliott may be selling the stuff to buy drugs and Glendon knows but doesn't want to face facts. We always know ten times more than we can put in the paper."

The torrent of gossip was alarming. What did Martha say about Ronald when he wasn't around?

CHAPTER FOUR

Ronald walked three blocks to the Miller County Courthouse. It had a Civil War soldier statue in front and framed paintings of county leaders going back to the nineteenth century on the lobby walls. Everybody who worked there was ancient. The elected clerk of court was a seventy-year-old country boy who shut himself in his office and talked on the phone all day. A dozen women did the real work. They were the ultimate grown-ups, unswerving in their dedication to order. They were suspicious of Ronald with his hippie hair, but they helped him search the public records on Lamont Moody. They found twelve debt collection lawsuits Lamont filed against customers of his equipment company and five speeding tickets. Nothing for drunk driving. Nothing on Archdale Street.

Ronald and Shelly, the new government reporter, went to dinner at McDonald's. She was in her late twenties, short, chunky, and had worn the same clothes every day that week: bell-bottom jeans, Beatle boots, and a black, ribbed turtleneck. She accessorized with a rotation of pendants on a chain necklace—a peace sign, the Venus symbol, a horse, and other animals.

"I don't own a dress. Not one," she said. "Okay, I still have my wedding dress, hanging in the closet wrapped in plastic, but I only wore it so my mother wouldn't have a heart attack. Steve didn't care. He would have been fine having a naked ceremony on a mountaintop. He's an atheist anyway. And a white dress! Are you kidding? I lost my virginity when I was fifteen. To Dickie Burgess on my living room sofa while my parents were asleep down the hall. But sometimes you do the traditional thing to keep the peace."

On her first day, Shelly went to cover the Miller County Commission, sat down in the meeting room, and took notes for an hour before realizing she was in the wrong courthouse in the wrong county. When she arrived at the right meeting, it was breaking up. She trailed a talkative commissioner into the parking lot, and he told her what happened. Her first story said Turner Kincaid, a Democrat, cast the lone vote against awarding a road-paving contract. The regulations attached to the federal grant, he said, were much like the abuses the US government inflicted on the south during Reconstruction. Kincaid telephoned Shelly, his voice roaring through the mouthpiece. Not only was he not a Democrat, he was the chairman of the county Republican Party. Shelly's story caused him to suffer ridicule at the coffee shop where he met his cronies every morning to discuss world events. Shelly went to the bathroom to cry and came back in ten minutes calling Kincaid a neo-Confederate Nazi Klansman. The correction was brief. Shelly's hatred of Turner Kincaid was permanent.

Ronald briefed her on office politics and warned her to beware the treachery of Linda Lasseter. Linda had hoped to get the government beat, but instead Mr. Carlton hired Shelly.

"I'm not worried about that bitch," Shelly said. She launched into a tale of surviving newsroom intrigue at her last job, at a tri-weekly in upstate South Carolina. She'd quit when her husband, Steve, got a reporting job at the Greensboro daily. The idea of being married to a fellow reporter intrigued Ronald. You could talk shop after sex.

They finished their Big Macs and went to the Millerton City Council meeting—Shelly to cover it and Ronald to observe Lamont Moody in the flesh. The council normally met on Monday, but this was a special meeting called on Friday afternoon to hear a request by Chief Smithers. They walked into the meeting room as people milled about, and Ronald bumped into a man.

"Excuse me there, buddy," the man said. "Don't think we've met. Lamont Moody."

Lamont was around fifty and wore the uniform of an aging frat boy: navy blazer with a light-blue shirt, red-striped tie, creased khaki pants, and black tassel loafers. He was handsome in a deteriorating way, with a thatch of white hair, a drooping mustache of darker color, and jowls starting to sag. He smelled like English Leather cologne and tobacco with an undertone of whiskey. No horns coming out of his head. They shook hands.

"Ronald Truluck from *The Eagle*," Ronald said.

Lamont arched an eyebrow and delivered a roguish, crooked smile.

"The Eaglet, huh? I read it every morning. I like to start my day with a laugh." Then he walked away to take his place as the meeting started.

The council met in the city courtroom, which had pews for spectators, like a church. Council members sat behind long tables in front of the elevated spot where the judge sat. Joe Stoneman, a hulking town cop with a whispered reputation for beating up handcuffed suspects, stood in the back to suppress citizen rebellion. Ronald nodded—they'd met at the police station—but Stoneman didn't nod back.

"Lamont's a creep," Shelly whispered as the clerk read the minutes of the last meeting. "I've known a thousand guys like him."

"Don't tell anybody I'm investigating him. I'm pretty sure Lamont knows from the look he gave me, and I only got the tip a few hours ago."

"He's a lot worse than a drunk driver. I can tell he's done something terrible. I think he's murdered people."

"That's a prejudicial thing to say," Ronald whispered, citing a phrase he picked up in journalism school. "Do you have any evidence?"

"I can smell the corruption coming off his body. He makes me want to puke."

"That's kind of opinionated."

"But it's true."

The meeting started with a prayer by a Boy Scout. Ronald kept his eyes open during the prayer and mouthed the words to the Pledge of Allegiance. He was agnostic and thought it was wrong for the council to even have a prayer or the Pledge.

Danny Tarlton, the doughboy city manager, ran the meeting. Mayor Stick, dressed in a white shirt, white pants with a white belt and white shoes, wisecracked throughout. When a council member pointed out that Stick forgot to call for a vote on one item, he replied, "Sounds like you've been studying *Roger's Rules of Orders*."

"Stick's an idiot. He gets everything wrong," Shelly whispered.

Chief Smithers stood to present a proposal for a new, stand-alone police station.

"You know how cramped we are in the current police station," he said. "The evidence room is too small, and we don't have a good place to fingerprint suspects. The current facility is not reflective of the quality of the Millerton Police Department. The council needs to approve a feasibility study for a new police headquarters. I know the council voted against the idea earlier, but you need to reconsider."

"Are you asking or demanding?" Stick said.

"I'm requesting," Smithers said.

"And how much is this Taj Mahal going to cost the taxpayers?"

"That's what the feasibility study would determine."

"How much would the study cost?"

"You'd need to take bids to find out."

Stick turned to the city manager. "Is this the way you do things in the city? Study everything to death?"

"It's standard procedure, Mayor," Danny Tarlton said.

"That doesn't seem like a very efficient way to do things," Stick said, shaking his head.

"Stick hates Danny," Shelly whispered. "He wants to get him fired. Danny's a creep too, but at least he's competent."

They didn't see or hear Stoneman, the cop, approach from behind. "Don't talk during the meeting," he whispered to them, but with such volume the action of the meeting stopped. Everybody looked at Stoneman, who was impossible to ignore. He was six-foot-six with a Marine Corps tattoo on his forearm.

"We're not disturbing anything," Shelly whispered back. "You're the one causing the disturbance."

"Miss, please calm down or I'll have to remove you from the meeting," Stoneman said, not whispering now. To Ronald he said, "You too, Eagle."

After Stoneman went to the back of the room, Stick said to the chief, "We've already said no to this once, Jim. Money's tight and the council doesn't want to raise taxes. There's no need to vote."

Lamont spoke up for the first time. "Mayor, the chief is correct about the condition of the station. It's a disgrace. It's disrespectful to the people of Millerton. And just because we conduct the feasibility study doesn't mean we're committing to building a new station, you know. I call for a vote to take bids for the study."

"That's not what you said last time," Stick said, glaring at Lamont. "You said it would cost too much."

"I've changed my mind," Lamont said. "You should try doing that now and then."

Lamont got a second and the motion passed three to two, with Stick casting one of the negative votes. Chief Smithers nodded at Lamont and sat down. The city attorney, Arthur Fleetwood Sr., started talking about revisions to regulations on sewer line extensions. The discussion was sleep inducing. Ronald felt like a heavy blanket had been dropped on his head. Lamont lifted his index finger in farewell as Ronald walked out of the council chambers.

Night had fallen. He'd driven four blocks when the lights activated on the police cruiser behind him. Wide awake now, Ronald jerked the Galaxie to the shoulder of the street, cut the engine, and pulled out his driver's license. Had Chief Smithers sent a brute to drag Ronald into the police station and torture him with rubber hoses and Barry Manilow music until he confessed to something? The cop had gotten out of his car and stood just outside Ronald's range of vision. All Ronald could see in his side mirror was a black leather belt holding a pistol holster, handcuffs, and other instruments of police violence.

"You're exceeding the speed limit, Eagle," Joe Stoneman said.

"Why did you leave the council meeting, Joe?"

"Driver's license."

Ronald hadn't been speeding but knew better than to argue with a cop on a dark street. He placed his license into Stoneman's meaty palm. Stoneman clicked on a flashlight to read the details.

"I've arrested a guy at your address last year. A pitiful drunk," Stoneman said. "You live in a dump with a bunch of pitiful drunks."

"They're not drunks; they're working men, the backbone of America."

Stoneman leaned down, putting his head level with Ronald's, and exhaled his hot breath into the car. Even in the dark, Ronald could see an angled scar on his lower lip. The cop reached into the car and slapped the license down hard on the dashboard.

"You've got a bad attitude, Eagle. You need to correct that, understand? This time, I'm giving you a break."

Ronald mumbled a thank you. He waited for Stoneman to drive away before he restarted his car.

CHAPTER FIVE

When he got home, Ronald went into the bathroom and smoked half a joint with the door shut, to keep anybody in the building from smelling the smoke. Then he turned the volume all the way down on his portable television, dropped a Grateful Dead concert album on the turntable, put on earphones, and flopped onto the sofa with nubby fabric. Sometimes, when he achieved a proper buzz, the world became synchronized. A drum rimshot on the record coincided with a cop firing a pistol into a bad guy's gut on TV, or a furious guitar solo began at the moment a pioneer woman wailed because the Indians scalped her husband.

But the sync didn't come. He was too frazzled after Stoneman's threat. He was sweating and jittery. Stoneman could have pulled him out of the car and pounded him into the pavement with the flashlight, then claimed Ronald started the fight. What had Ronald done to anger a big cop? Was it a routine exertion of police power for the sake of intimidation, or was there a deeper warning?

He removed the earphones and walked around his apartment. He lived in one room in a drafty, wood frame house subdivided into six living spaces.

The advertisement said furnished, and because Millerton had furniture factories, he imagined gleaming wooden chairs and tables. But the old chairs creaked, the table wobbled, and the fabric on the sofa gave him a rash. He had a two-burner gas stove, a chest-high refrigerator his landlord called an icebox, and a Murphy bed. The bed sold Ronald on the apartment. It was a novelty. He'd seen one on a television show about New York City, but never in real life. It really was a dump—worse than any place he lived in college, but all he could afford on one hundred ten dollars a week. His neighbors were mill workers, single men who sat on the front steps smoking and drinking beer. Ronald nodded when he came and went, but they just stared. He was an alien.

Ronald wasn't prepared for mill town life. He grew up in Cary, a suburb of Raleigh, the state capital. His father was a dentist, and his mother kept the house and read books all day. Ronald never paid attention to the rough edges of life. He lived in a cocoon of self-absorption with his head buried in books, comics, and music. He never set foot in a factory, a police station, or a city council meeting. He avoided talking to poor people. Now he had to do it every day.

In college, he majored in marijuana and minored in journalism, because writing came easy. Then Watergate happened. Journalism became something besides the career path of least resistance. It became a noble crusade. Like all the other J-school students in the country, he was going to bring down the enemies of democracy while maintaining a permanent high. But after graduation, Ronald couldn't get an interview with a single paper, much less a job. He had zero work experience. He appealed to a professor who made a call. Ronald was invited to talk with I.J. Carlton at *The Eagle,* a six-day-a-week paper with a 3,000 circulation. Ronald had never heard of it.

He showed up for the interview stoned, wearing his penny loafers, a navy-blue blazer, and a paisley tie borrowed from his father. Everybody looked up when he stepped into the newsroom and Ronald thought, "These are the ugliest adults I've ever seen." His hair was longer than anybody except the young woman who buttoned her blouse tight at the neck. He knew he'd never hang out with her; her desk was much too neat. An older woman with a tight hairstyle held a phone to her ear and smiled, as if the person on the other end could see her. Ronald realized with alarm he might be working with somebody like his mother.

A man stood behind his desk and motioned for Ronald to come on over, though he seemed uncomfortable with the idea. He looked uncomfortable, period. He had an eyepatch. Why hadn't somebody told Ronald about the eyepatch?

Mr. Carlton looked through Ronald's writing samples and read aloud a feature from a J-school class: "'When Alex Jenkins told campus police his bike was stolen from the student union, he was told he'd joined a club that included three hundred students a year.'" He said to Ronald, "The college has a club for people who have their bikes stolen? What are the dues?"

Ronald scanned the room and locked eyes with a grinning troll-like head covered by a bowl haircut. This, said a placard with block lettering thumbtacked to the wall, was Snap Tolbert, Sports Editor. The wall around Snap was covered with glossy black-and-white pictures of rock musicians and a poster for a band named Blue Smoke.

"That's a figure of speech," Ronald said to Mr. Carlton. "The school has a lot of clubs—debate club, drama club. They even have a golf club." No reaction, no smile. "They don't have a bike theft club."

"Well, we wouldn't use that figure of speech at this paper," Mr. Carlton said, as if *The Eagle* had the highest journalistic standards in the land. After five more minutes of halting conversation, he said, "Let me think about this."

Ronald left the interview chastened, but Mr. Carlton called the next day and offered him the police reporter job, asking him to commit to giving *The Eagle* a year of his life. Ronald jumped on the Watergate train, even if he was riding in the caboose. Later, Snap told Ronald that Mr. Carlton had to hire somebody in a hurry. The previous police reporter quit without giving notice to drive a bread truck, a job that paid more money.

Ronald sat down at his kitchen table and picked up an old copy of *The Eagle*. "Vandals Paint Obscenities on High School Lockers," read the headline on his story. Underneath the picture of workmen painting over dirty words ran an editorial in which Mr. Carlton decried vandalism and blamed it on bad parenting. Mr. Carlton attacked weak targets but not somebody who could push back, like Lamont Moody or Chief Smithers. Ronald was different. He wasn't afraid.

Something from the council meeting knocked around inside his head. Lamont had cocked his head and looked right at Ronald. Made fun of *The Eagle*. Walked away without saying goodbye. It was an insult. What was Ronald going to do about it?

He went to the bathroom mirror. His attempted beard was pitiful, more like adolescent pubic hair. No wonder nobody respected him. Ronald lathered up and shaved. When he wiped away the foam, a new face—indeed, a whole new person—looked back.

Ronald made a silent promise to himself. Lamont Moody would not flick him away with his index finger. To expose unethical behavior, Ronald had to be hyper-ethical himself. Pure. His personal and professional worlds would never overlap. If he alienated friends, so what? From this moment forward, he would be a truth-speaking journalist on and off the job. To seal the vow, he smoked the other half of the joint.

CHAPTER SIX

The next day, Ronald tried on three shirts in front of the bathroom mirror. He decided on the Grateful Dead T-shirt. It was a cultural statement that would help him make small talk at Shelly's party. His lace-up work boots, purchased that morning at the Army-Navy surplus store, completed his ensemble. He stashed six joints in a baggie underneath his spare tire.

It was a thirty-minute drive from Millerton to Greensboro, one of the state's big cities. Dusk had settled over Shelly and Steve's neighborhood when Ronald arrived. Oak Grove Plantation encapsulated the suburbs in every soul-shrinking detail. Kids on bikes. Lawns, mowed and trimmed. A father figure with a crew cut washing his Plymouth in the driveway. Had Ronald misjudged Shelly? Was she a suburbanite posing as a bohemian?

He parked behind a Chevy Corvair with a McGovern bumper sticker. Shelly's yard was a mess. A rusty rake lay with its tongs pointed up. He had to step over a pool-cue-sized tree limb on the sidewalk. Two empty beer bottles stood sentinel on either side of the wide-open front door. In the smoky living room, manic voices mixed into one high-pitched roar, underlaid with Otis Redding pleading for love. Everybody was older, some by twenty years. Nobody wore a T-shirt.

"Ronald!" Shelly shrieked and bounced barefoot across the shag carpet. This being the weekend, she wore a white turtleneck instead of a black turtleneck with a peace sign pendant. They hugged and she said, "Let me get you a beer."

The kitchen was tight with bodies. A woman with a pixie haircut gesticulated with wild hand motions. A languid Black guy shrugged in response. Uncorked liquor bottles lined the counter, none of it the cheap stuff. Two men in their thirties, both with well-tended facial hair, blocked the refrigerator door and argued about who was the most corrupt president in history— Nixon or Andrew Johnson.

Their conversation thrilled Ronald. They weren't talking about car engines or what happened in high school or how many times they puked last weekend. Shelly opened the refrigerator and placed a cold metal cylinder into Ronald's right palm. The anticipatory first-beer feeling spread through his body. He wanted to tell Shelly she was right to take full responsibility for the error about the county commissioner but she'd disappeared.

He drifted into the living room full of strangers. On the wall next to the kitchen entrance hung a framed, formal wedding photo. Shelly looked wide open to the future in her white dress. Her husband Steve had unruly hair he'd tried to plaster down, a craggy face, and slitted, snaky eyes.

"Five years ago," a voice rasped next to Ronald's ear. The flesh-and-blood Steve stood two feet away, holding a beer and sneer-smiling. His breast pocket bulged with a pack of Camels, a ball point pen, and a folded sheet of paper. "It was hot as hell. I couldn't wait to get out of that monkey suit. If you ever get married, don't do it in July in Greensboro."

"I don't even have a girlfriend. I'm Ronald. I work with Shelly at *The Eagle*."

"I know. She told me your paper had two people who were real journalists and that you're one of them."

Who was the other real journalist? Martha or Mr. Carlton? They shook and Ronald said, "Let's get stoned."

In the backyard they stood on the edge of a brick patio, alone in the darkness except for a couple whispering by the wooden fence. Ronald lit the joint, toked, and handed it to Steve. Steve took a deep toke that burned down a quarter of the joint. It was like watching a time-progression film of the ocean tide going out. He exhaled a thin jet stream toward the sky and said, "What are you working on?"

Ronald toked, held, exhaled, and explained Lamontgate.

"This Lamont guy didn't get charged with drunk driving, did he?" Steve said

"The cops let him off. They buried the accident report."

"And the homeowners won't talk? That's weird."

"The wife will never talk. She hates me. Her husband wants to tell me something, but his wife won't let him. One of my editors, Martha, had a run-in with the guy a few years ago. She says he's unreliable and doesn't want to put him in the paper in any way."

"You need to get some cops to talk," Steve said. "Or an ex-cop."

"Would they be reliable sources? Wouldn't they just be seeking revenge?"

"Of course, they'd be seeking revenge."

"What are you working on?" Ronald asked to be polite.

A Greensboro councilman had voted against tightening the city's massage parlor ordinance without revealing he was part owner in three massage parlors, including the infamous Korean Baths, where an undercover cop got stabbed by a masseuse and almost died.

"And you know who gave me the tip?" Steve said. "The undercover cop who got stabbed. Then I just followed a paper trail to the councilman. Pissed off cops are the best sources."

Ronald smoked all his joints with new friends he'd never see again and opened his eyes the next morning, lying on the sofa, covered by an afghan and still wearing his boots. Beer cans and empty glasses occupied every flat surface in the living room. He hoped Shelly and Steve would wake up and fix breakfast. His dry mouth compelled him to go to the kitchen sink and drink four glasses of water. He found aspirin in the bathroom, then went back to the kitchen and drank more water. When he turned the Galaxie's key, the roar of the engine broke the neighborhood's Sunday morning stillness.

CHAPTER
SEVEN

Ronald didn't have time for Lamontgate when he went back to work on Monday. Breaking news intervened: an armed robbery at Prescott's Beverage Mart. This robbery was a blow against traditional sex roles. Two young women wearing tank tops demanded not only cash, but Chapstick, four cartons of menthol cigarettes, and a bag of chewing tobacco. One of them fired three rounds into the beer coolers with a short-barreled black revolver. They ran out the door howling and escaped in a green pickup truck driven by a man with long blond hair.

"The one with the gun had a fantastic figure and big brown puppy dog eyes," clerk Johnnie Youngblood told Ronald. "I didn't mind getting robbed by them."

"Weren't you afraid of getting killed?" Ronald said.

"Nah. If you don't piss 'em off, they won't shoot your ass." Johnnie belonged to the league of convenience store heroes who braved snow, rain, and bullets to keep the world stocked in beer and cigarettes.

When he got back to the office, Ronald wrote: "Johnnie Youngblood, a veteran of robberies, having been held up Oct. 14 while clerking at the Bob's

Convenience Store at 444 Ammons Road; Jan. 22 while behind the counter at the Hess Station at 23 Christmas St.; and March 7 at the Grab and Go Store at 212 Grab and Go Road, said he never feared the gun-brandishing woman would pump bullets into his body.

"'If you don't make them angry,' Youngblood said, 'they won't shoot you.'"

Ronald sanitized the "ass" out of the quote, knowing not to offend *The Eagle* readership. He ended the story with Johnnie sweeping up glass shards glistening in the afternoon sunlight. That image was captured on film by Lewis who, as always, arrived at the crime scene well before Ronald.

Ronald then told Mr. Carlton and Martha about being pulled over by Joe Stoneman after the city council meeting. "I wasn't speeding," he said. "I wasn't."

"The guy's just throwing his weight around," Mr. Carlton said. "You got off with a warning. He didn't hit you or anything ..."

"It's police harassment. It may have something to do with the questions I was asking about Lamont Moody."

"You haven't found out anything about Lamont, so I think you need to calm down," Martha said. They weren't serious about getting Lamont.

When he finished work, Ronald found Snap Tolbert, the sports editor, waiting in the parking lot. Ronald had endured Snap's monologues about the star potential of his weekend rock band, Blue Smoke, but they'd never had a real conversation. Snap was starting a soul patch under his lower lip, the trademark of Greg Allman, the prince of southern rock.

"So you're working on a story about Lamont," Snap said. "I'll help."

"Does he drink a lot?"

"Like a fish. Like a gigantic fish. Like a whale."

"Whales are mammals, not fish."

"Whatever. Let's get a beer and maybe we'll run into Lamont, and you can ask him questions while he's drunk. You drive."

As they moved through the mean streets of Millerton, Snap filled in Ronald about their coworkers. Mr. Carlton lost his eye when he fell out of a tree as a boy. It kept him out of the army during World War II. His son was a big druggie who dropped out of college. Martha used to work as an assistant metro editor for *The Guardian* in Winston-Salem, the city built on cigarettes. She quit when she was demoted to reporter, ostensibly because of a headline error. Snap heard it was because of a bad breakup with her married boyfriend, an assistant managing editor. Linda Lasseter was a drip in high school and was a drip now. The women's editor, Anne Richmond, was a sweetheart.

Their first stop was The Food Mart, which used to be a grocery store. Now it sold beer and foods to facilitate the drinking of beer, like chips, nuts, and beef jerky. Also, bags of ice, coolers, cigarettes, snuff, rolling papers, and some fishing gear. Snap got two sixteen-ounce Budweisers from the cooler and put them on the counter.

"Horace, were you working the night Lamont wrecked on Archdale Street?" he asked the man behind the counter.

"Nope, I was in the hospital sitting with my wife after she had bowel surgery," Horace said. He was about sixty with a basketball-sized belly that stretched his polyester golf shirt. Everybody in town had heard about the wreck.

"Maybe the guys in back will know," Snap said. He gestured to the beers and said to Ronald, "You can get the next round."

They went through a screen door. A dozen men were drinking beer and smoking while standing on a patch of parking lot hidden from the street by the dumpster and a battered privacy fence. The drinkers dropped their voices when they saw Ronald, a stranger. Snap introduced him to a guy in a hunting cap, Reggie, and everybody went back to talking.

Ronald ripped off the pop top and detected the carbonated hiss of a deflowered malt beverage. He took a deep swallow. It tasted so good he couldn't stop himself from saying, "That's good." It was an indisputably true statement. He inhaled the cigarette smoke, the beer, the dumpster stench, the car exhaust from the street, the asphalt, the animal manure on Reggie's boots. It was a magnificent stink, emanating from the spot where he stood and not concocted in his imagination. It was a parking lot epiphany.

"Beer *is* good," Reggie agreed. He told a joke about four people having sex in an airplane bathroom but couldn't remember the punchline, then transitioned into a story about losing his best five-eighths-inch wrench on a truck engine repair job. Reggie was real but his story bored Ronald. He excused himself and found Snap.

"Where are we? Is this a bar?"

"More like a club, or a bunch of guys drinking beer in somebody's backyard, except we're doing it in the back of a store. It's cool."

"But a package store and a bar need different kinds of licenses. Do the police know this is going on?"

"I don't know about licenses, but I see cops in here all the time. And councilmen."

The local authorities had a pick-and-choose attitude about when to enforce the law. Before he could ask another question, a man in a gray herringbone blazer sauntered up and shook Snap's hand and then Ronald's. He was the nattiest drinker in the parking lot, with a loosened tie and glowing black hair that was slicked straight back. The Food Mart had sartorial democracy.

"Ronald Truluck of *The Eagle*, meet Harold Jameson," Snap said.

"Just like the whiskey," Jameson croaked. He put his left hand on Snap's shoulder to steady himself and drained his can of Miller High Life.

"Jameson used to be on the city council, but Lamont won his seat a few years ago," Snap said. "You were a good councilman, Jameson. How long did you serve?"

"Eight years. Did some good things. Those new basketball goals at Curry Park? That was my idea. I got the tennis courts resurfaced. Did anybody say thank you?"

"We're looking for Lamont," Snap said.

"I haven't seen Lamont in two weeks and I'm glad of it. I don't like being around him. Whenever our paths cross, he reminds me he beat me. He just won by twelve votes."

"Did you hear about his car wreck?" Ronald said.

Jameson inspected Ronald. He didn't like being questioned by a stranger. Ronald tightened his mouth to emit trustworthiness. He had a habit of letting it hang open in moments of repose.

"Are you talking about the wreck on Archdale Street?" Jameson said. "How'd you hear about it?"

"A source. I can't say who."

Jameson nodded, as if withholding information was the way his world operated. "What else?"

"Nobody wants to talk to me about it. Not the police and not the people who live in the house where he wrecked."

"Typical," Jameson said. "Stuff gets covered up all the time in Millerton."

"Why are the police covering it up?"

"Couple of reasons," Jameson said. A car with a sputtering muffler passed by on the street, forcing Ronald and Snap to lean in to hear. "Lamont got a DUI in Raleigh last year he couldn't wiggle out of. If he gets another one and a prosecutor plays it by the book, Lamont could lose his driver's license."

"You think he's paying off Chief Smithers?" Ronald said. "Or does it have something to do with the new police station?"

"Bingo. The chief wants to get a brand-new police station built but he's not getting full support from the council. Stick is fighting the idea for some reason. So the chief is covering up Lamont's wreck to make sure Lamont goes along with his plan. And from what I hear, Lamont is playing ball."

"I was at the meeting. Lamont made a motion for the feasibility study."

"Good man—you're doing your homework," Jameson said. "I'm glad to see somebody at *The Eagle* has a sense of outrage. Your boss, I.J. Carlton, looks the other way for everything. If you want to know more about that wreck, you should talk to Dwight Bennett."

"Who's he?" Ronald said.

"A cop," Snap said.

"He used to be a cop," Jameson said. "He just got fired."

An ex-cop. The best kind of source, according to Steve. But would he be an honest source? Someone with integrity?

"The official reason Dwight got canned is he wasn't following a procedure or hadn't filled out some paperwork or something like that," Jameson said. "But the real reason is he was having an affair with Stick's daughter."

"Cynthia? I thought she was engaged," Snap said.

"She's engaged in deceit," intoned Jameson, a scholar of infidelity.

Snap and Jameson condemned Cynthia's faithlessness then appraised her figure, which they ranked above average.

"One thing I don't get," Ronald said. "The chief doesn't like Stick and Stick doesn't like the chief. Why would the chief do a favor for the mayor and fire Dwight?"

"Politics don't always make sense," Jameson said. "The chief and Stick do hate each other, but the chief is trying to win favor with Stick so he'll change his mind on the police station. The problem is, Stick is too damn dumb to understand how the game is played. He doesn't understand a damn thing."

CHAPTER EIGHT

"I can't believe Dwight got fired just for sleeping with Cynthia," Snap said as they drove to the next bar. "He's already broken every rule in the policy manual."

"How did he get away with it?"

"Dwight's a local guy who was a football star at Millerton High. And he's a Vietnam combat vet. People respect that, including the chief."

"Who told you about Dwight breaking all those rules? I'd like to pursue that story."

"Somebody I ran into last week, but we were just talking."

Just talking. That meant this is the good stuff but off the record by unspoken agreement. How to get that information on the record was the challenge. Whenever Ronald went into reporter mode and pulled out a notepad, people froze up.

It was dark now. Snap pulled out a joint and lit up. Ronald tensed. Smoking dope on the bypass was one thing, but he'd promised himself not to partake of intoxicants in a vehicle at night in the Millerton city limits. Getting arrested would be unprofessional. On the other hand, he loved to smoke dope in cars while listening to loud music. It was cheap, didn't require much effort, and provided unintended metaphysical benefits. If he was riding down the road in a fast car listening to a song about riding down the road in a fast car, his inner and outer worlds synchronized. Art became life. He took the joint.

It was loosely rolled and bulged in the middle, then narrowed down to the inhaling end. It burned fast because the marijuana was not evenly distributed. A little stick poked through the paper. Ronald's joints were works of art—smooth and tapered. He cleaned out sticks and seeds by pushing the marijuana around on one of his album covers. He took a medium-sized toke of Snap's joint and judged it to be cheap Mexican marijuana—rough on the throat and providing a short-term high.

Their next stop was a flat-topped building just inside the city limits. The walls were unadorned cinder block except for a painted square announcing the club's name, Exiles on Main Street, after the Rolling Stones' overrated double album. The building vibrated with jukebox music. Ronald had written several cop briefs about marijuana arrests and a girl fight at Exiles.

He and Snap passed through a gauntlet of long hairs leaning against pickup trucks and hotrods—Camaros, Firebirds, and GTOs with spoilers, hood scoops, and silver exhaust pipes. No VW hippie vans. Everybody was smoking a cigarette, lighting a cigarette, bumming a cigarette, or rubbing one out with their shoe. Ronald felt like they were classifying him as a straight. Why? Because he drove a beige car and wore a button-down dress shirt from work. Ronald sensed menace. Rednecks used to have short hair. But after the Allman Brothers came along, rednecks grew their hair long and birthed a new breed of white male: Headnecks. Beneath the car leaners' nonchalance was an edge, the suggestion things could go bad if Ronald said the wrong thing. Peace, love, and fuck you.

Inside the bar, the jukebox played "Gimme Three Steps," a southern rock anthem about almost getting shot in a bar. A girl whooped, and guys laughed at the foosball table. At a corner booth, a drunk in a tank top snored with his head tossed back. They made their way through the darkness to the bar and Ronald ordered two bottles of Budweiser.

"Can't do it," the bartender said. "We only serve beer in plastic cups. It cuts down on the broken glass."

A power ballad came out of the jukebox. Ronald and Snap conversed in almost normal voices during the whimpering, acoustic intro. Snap said he might quit the newspaper because journalism prevented him from developing Blue Smoke's full artistic potential. The song approached its crashing, metallic orgasm, and Ronald couldn't understand another word. He knew Snap was griping so he yelled, "That sucks." Snap nodded in appreciation and bought two more beers.

Three girls walked up. All of them had long straight hair parted straight down the middle to create a white line of exposed scalp that bisected their heads. Ronald, stoned, considered saying, "Hey, if you're ever subjected to psychological testing, your hairstyles would help scientists identify your left brain and right brain functions." But he couldn't remember which side of the brain was for logical pursuits and which side was for writing novels, so he said nothing.

Snap made the introductions. Chris had a hook nose and wore dangling earrings with turquoise stones. Judy was bony, with fatalistic eyes and bad posture. Monica wore Gloria Steinem aviator glasses, a little makeup, and a Joni Mitchell T-shirt. She looked older than the others, maybe twenty-five, and was better groomed. She didn't have split ends like Ronald and every other customer in the bar.

Ronald offered to buy beers. Monica said, "A white wine would be fine."

"This is a beer joint. They don't sell wine," he said.

"I should have known." She waved cigarette smoke away from her face.

Snap held an imaginary joint to his lips and mimicked puffing. Judy said to Monica, "We're going out back to smoke pot."

"I'll go with you because I don't want to stand around here by myself and get accosted by some creep, but I don't smoke pot or anything else," Monica said. "It's bad for your lungs."

The group walked through the back door and onto a concrete pad. The smell of something burning hung in the air and broken glass crackled under their shoes. Ronald began composing a cop brief: "Intoxicated reporter arrested behind local tavern." They moved into a shadow and a joint made the rounds. Monica passed it without taking a hit.

"I need this," Judy said. "I had a big fight with my mother about Elliott."

"Where is Elliott anyway?" Chris said.

"He's working at his stepfather's hardware store doing inventory."

Could that be the Elliott who Martha described? The unnamed suspect in petty thefts from the ex-mayor's house? The wall Ronald hoped to build between his professional and private lives was crumbling.

"Snap says you work with him at *The Eagle*," Chris said to Ronald.

"The Eaglet!" Judy said. "The Sparrow, The Buzzard, The Penguin, The Ostrich."

"I had no idea the paper was so well respected," he said. "I'm the police reporter."

"The Millerton cops are dirty," Judy said. "They busted Elliott for possession of marijuana and I'm positive they planted dope in his car. Elliott is too smart to do something like leave a bag of dope on the floorboard for anybody to see."

"That sounds exactly like something Elliott would do," Snap said.

"Remember when Elliott was seventeen and he broke into that house and realized he'd lost his wallet," Chris said. "So he broke into it again to see if he'd left it there, and that's when the people came home. And it turned out he'd forgotten his wallet on top of his dresser at home."

"He did do that," Judy admitted. To Ronald she said, "Next time you see Dwight Bennett, tell him he's a real son of a bitch. He's the one who busted Elliott."

"Will do," Ronald said. Another mention of Dwight Bennett. Was that a cosmic signal?

"Where'd you go to college?" Monica said. Nobody in Millerton had asked that. Higher education was not on most people's minds.

"Chapel Hill. Journalism."

"I was accepted at Chapel Hill but wanted to get far away from home," she said.

"Monica goes to Florida," Chris said. "She used to be my babysitter."

"I'm a grad student," Monica clarified. "English."

"I almost flunked English in high school," Judy said.

"I almost flunked it in college. That's why I dropped out," Chris added.

Judy and Chris didn't catch Monica's dismissive look, and they started gossiping with Snap about Millerton people they knew in common. Monica swung her attention to Ronald and said, "Do you own a gun? My father wanted to teach me how to shoot, but I said no way. Guns should be banned. People should have to turn in their guns. If they don't, the government should go inside their houses and search for them. If somebody is caught with a gun, they should go to prison for a long time. Even cops shouldn't be allowed to have guns. We'd have less crime, less violence. Less death. Don't you think so?"

The idea was idiotic, but her question poked a hibernating section of his brain. Since moving to Millerton, he hadn't heard anyone express a thought unrelated to the problem right in front of them. Snap, for instance, had once wished somebody would invent a solar car, not because it would save the planet but because he didn't have enough cash to buy a full tank of gas. Millerton was ruled by the tyranny of the real.

"I don't think that would be a workable idea," Ronald said. "And no, I don't have a gun."

The jukebox stopped and the group moved toward the door. The lights had been turned on inside and revealed the naked squalor of closing time. A pair of men's underpants lay on top of a Formica table. Cigarette butts floated in ashtrays filled with yellowish liquid that might be beer. The bartender swept plastic cups into a pile. In the parking lot, headnecks finished their beers. A police car rolled by, and they hid their cups beside their legs, like the cops didn't know.

Chris, Judy, and Snap resumed their conversation about something somebody said about somebody they all knew—the tiniest of small talk. Monica looked at Ronald as they stood under the orange glow of the streetlight in the parking lot. He looked at her.

"Would you like to get together and talk about guns some more?" Ronald asked.

"Let's pick another subject," she said. "Something besides guns and football."

"How about books? I read one in college."

She laughed. Ronald swelled with a sense of well-being. To achieve happiness, he needed a girl to laugh at his jokes. That seemed attainable.

Snap tried to convince the girls into going to his house to smoke more dope but Chris had to work in the morning, or said she did. They drove away in a Chevy Impala with a deep dent in the passenger door, Judy behind the wheel, Chris riding shotgun, and Monica in back.

CHAPTER NINE

According to the clipboard at the police department, Millerton was reeling from a wave of hubcap thefts. Ronald wrote down details while Betty Stokes stood by exhaling noxious fumes.

"Anything new with our friend Lamont?" he asked. That showed he was following her tip.

"Nope. But did you hear about Dwight Bennett?"

Here came a poker-hand conversation in which Betty didn't reveal everything she knew. Jameson did the same thing at The Food Mart. Did they do it for deniability, or for a sense of power over Ronald? Trying to play the game himself, Ronald said, "Didn't hear that."

"Let's just say he's no longer employed by the Millerton Police Department."

"He got fired? What for?"

"I didn't say he was fired."

"He resigned?"

"Didn't say that either."

"What *are* you saying?"

"I'm just saying some high-ranking city officials are very happy right now. And Dwight is very unhappy."

He flipped through more reports and said, "I'd like to talk with Dwight, but I'm sure his phone number is unlisted."

She walked away, came back and laid a book of matches on the counter next to the clipboard. Outside city hall, Ronald opened the matchbook and found a phone number written in Betty's slanted handwriting. As soon as Ronald sat down at his desk, Linda marched over.

"You made a style error in the garage fire story," she said. "The fire captain's title is abbreviated as 'Capt.' Not like the thing you wear on your head."

"Says who?"

"*The Associated Press Stylebook.*"

That was the newsroom Bible, a collection of rules on how to abbreviate, hyphenate, and punctuate that Ronald intuitively violated. She flipped open the stylebook on his desk.

"This section shows you the proper abbreviations for each rank. It applies to police but is listed under military titles. That may be the reason you didn't look because I know you're anti-military."

In college everybody he knew was anti-military, except the ROTC guys. People in Millerton were different. He'd made a few cracks about Vietnam that caused Linda to stiffen. She returned to her dust-free desk, where every pen, pencil, paper clip, and piece of paper was positioned at right angles. A Miller County Community College associate's degree hung on the wall. Ronald dialed the number on the matchbook. Dwight answered on the second ring. Ronald introduced himself and said, "I hear you've left the employ of the Millerton police, Dwight."

"Who told you that?" The voice was gruff and twangy.

"A source I cannot reveal. Would you like to talk?"

"What the hell. Come on over." He gave his address and hung up.

Linda motored across the carpet like a robot in high gear. Her face was flushed.

"I heard you on the phone," she said. "Was that Dwight Bennett? He's a friend. Please tell me what you're going to talk to him about."

He told her Dwight lost his job. He gestured to the chair beside his desk and Linda sat with perfect posture. He put on a cop stoneface to see what effect it would have.

"My sister dated Dwight when they were in high school; that's how I know him," Linda jabbered. The stare was working. "He's a good guy. One time, he took Lorna to the county fair and invited me to come with them. I was in junior high. Lorna kind of made him do it, because Mother told her to, but he went along with it. Dwight and Lorna let me ride in the front seat with them. At the fair, he bought me an orange drink and cotton candy. He threw darts and won a prize and gave it to me. He didn't make fun of me for being a kid. Then ..."

"What kind of prize?" said Ronald, the interrogator.

"It was a stuffed tiger. I used to keep it on my bed, and now I keep it in a box of knickknacks in my closet, with some old school stuff. I named it Tony."

Like the Frosted Flakes commercials. Such a lame, unoriginal name. Why not Antonio? Ronald didn't put her down. This was the first time they'd talked without rancor.

"When he graduated, Dwight enlisted in the army and was sent to Vietnam. He came back alive, thank God. But when you ask him what happened in Vietnam, he says nothing happened, but something did. He's unhappy. He had a bad war experience. I think he needs help. The military can be hard on people. My father spent twenty-six years in the army. He served in the South Pacific in World War II and then in Korea. I was born at Fort Benning. Lorna too."

Ronald had no firsthand knowledge of the military. He got a high number in the draft lottery that put him out of reach. Not only did he avoid getting killed in Vietnam, he didn't have to decide whether to be a draft dodger. Without trying, he'd avoided the defining crisis of his generation.

"I'm going to talk with Dwight to see what I can dig up," he said. He didn't want her to know he was investigating Lamont Moody. She'd rat him out to Mr. Carlton if she knew.

As he gathered his notepad, pen, cigarettes, and car keys, Linda said, "If he's not at his apartment, you might check his mother's house on Table

Street. And his ex-wife and daughter live in the county, down Tar Pit Road. She drives a red Malibu with the antenna torn off."

"What happened to the antenna?"

"Her boyfriend was driving her car one night and got into a fight outside a hamburger joint. He ripped off the antenna and hit the other guy a couple of times in the face and then people broke it up. He was supposed to get it fixed but never did."

"Classy. What's the daughter's name?"

"Amber. His ex-wife is named Teresa Tyler Bennett. I know all this because my sister still kind of has a crush on Dwight."

"Just your sister?"

Linda returned to her typewriter, blushing.

CHAPTER TEN

Ronald parked outside Building C at Paradise Apartments. The address provoked sly chuckles in Millerton. This was where the town swingers frolicked. They played tennis at all hours on two lighted courts, grilled hamburgers on charcoal grills, and washed away their inhibitions in the oval blue swimming pool. College girls wore tiny bikinis. Guys drank beer from coolers. People made out in the shallow end of the pool. You could play the radio loud and nobody complained. Once a week the cops rousted skinny dippers at three in the morning.

Ronald had inquired about renting there and walked out shaking his head at the price. That's why he lived in a dump instead of Millerton's version of the Playboy Mansion.

When Dwight answered the door, he didn't project the mind-reading cop's eyeball. He didn't look at Ronald at all. He had a ruddy face and jutting chin that commanded attention when he wore a cop uniform, but in his T-shirt and gym shorts he looked puffy and tired.

The apartment was decorated in early American castoff. An apple crate served as an end table for a loveseat. Smoke and the smell of beer permeated the shag carpet. No woman lived in this apartment—the squalor proved that—but a whiff of perfume indicated one visited not long ago. Dwight walked into the kitchen, sighing like it took great effort. He put a pot of water on a burner and gazed out the window above the sink.

"Sorry about your job," Ronald said.

Mr. Carlton and Martha said Dwight distinguished himself by not doing anything stupid, like forgetting to put his patrol car into park and watching it roll down the boat ramp into Lake Miller, as did one of his colleagues. Dwight's top attribute was serving in Vietnam. The assumption was he'd killed people. That gave him a gravitas most Millerton police officers lacked.

Ronald backgrounded Dwight by looking through the yellowed clippings Mr. Carlton kept in envelopes in a file drawer. Two years ago, Dwight shot and wounded an armed robber running through a convenience store parking lot, though follow-up stories simply called him a robber. Mr. Carlton said it turned out the man didn't have a gun or knife or any other weapon, so he wasn't an *armed* robber. When Ronald asked why *The Eagle* never reported that fact or ran a correction, Mr. Carlton said it would have made people disrespect the police, and the bad guy had a long criminal history anyway. Later, Snap said Chief Smithers dropped into the office and asked Mr. Carlton to leave out the lack of a weapon.

Dwight kept staring out the window. "Do you have other work lined up?" Ronald said.

"What happened," Dwight said, "is Chief Smithers got wind I was stopping at Mama's house on lunch break during my shift to check on her dog while she's at work because the dog was about to drop a litter of puppies. The watch commander said it was okay for me to do that. That's the absolute my-hand-on-the-Bible truth."

"What kind of dog?" Ronald asked, since details made the story.

"But when Chief Smithers asked the watch commander, he lied and said he told me it was not okay, that I didn't have permission to check on the dog. They just wanted to get rid of me. I was screwed."

"What was the official reason they put on your discharge papers?"

"It's not about being a good cop. It's a popularity contest and I'm no good at that game. And now I may have to start working the graveyard shift at the blanket factory beside guys I've arrested. I'll be down at their level, and they'll be laughing at me. But I need a paycheck. I've got a four-year-old daughter to support, and my ex-wife can't keep a job."

The water boiled. Dwight spooned instant coffee into a mug for himself, poured in steaming water, and stirred. He sipped and looked out the window some more. Was he insulting Ronald by not offering coffee? Or was he a clueless rube?

"I heard you were fired because you were having an affair with the mayor's daughter," Ronald said. "Is that true?"

Dwight exhaled with force. His residual cop personality rose to the surface. He liked to ask questions, not answer them. "I can't believe somebody would say that," he said. Another non-denial denial.

Working with Dwight would be an ongoing power struggle. Dwight was better equipped to wage that battle because of his years spent bullying people while in uniform.

"You're wasting my time," Ronald said and walked out of the kitchen.

"I can give you the accident report on Lamont Moody," Dwight called when Ronald reached the front door. "I know that's what you're looking for."

Ronald walked back. Dwight picked up his coffee mug and strode to a dining room table. He sat and patted the table twice, a wordless summons. That rubbed Ronald wrong.

"If I ask you a question, you give me an honest answer. No lies. Okay?"

"What are you talking about? Have you been smoking wacky weed already?"

How did Dwight know? An educated guess? Or did Ronald's demeanor scream out stoner? He sat.

"This is what I can do," Dwight said. "I can get you a copy of the accident report. You won't find it in any public file because it's still 'under investigation' and will be forever because the chief is covering up for Lamont."

"That's a good start."

"A good start? That's the whole damn story. Lamont ran off the road at two in the morning and plowed into the front yard of Bill Jorgensen's house. No charges. Another cop showed up at the wreck scene and took Lamont away. Then the accident report was buried."

"Who was the other cop?"

"Joe Stoneman."

Ronald didn't like Joe Stoneman being involved in any way. He'd been giving Ronald dirty looks at the police station.

"Who wrote the accident report?" Ronald said. "I need to interview the officer."

Dwight tapped his chest with two fingers. He beamed. No wonder he was acting so high and mighty. Ronald needed him above all other sources.

"Why didn't you say so? That's great," Ronald said. They were partners now. "Did you smell alcohol on Lamont's breath?"

"Yes, and I saw beer cans and liquor bottles on the floor of the car."

"Incredible. I can't believe he got away with this. You put that in the accident report, didn't you?"

Dwight shook his head. Ronald grimaced. Having the alcohol documented would make Lamont's crime more heinous.

"Why not? I see that kind of thing on accident reports all the time."

"Because I had the feeling they'd cover up for Lamont because he's on the city council. That's how things work in a small town like Millerton. I didn't know they'd bury the whole accident report. How does the chief repay me for being a team player? He fires my ass."

Dwight's credibility dipped. He tried to cover up a crime. But he was the kind of source Ronald needed: a pissed-off ex-cop.

"When can I get this accident report?" Ronald said.

"In a couple of days. I'll call and let you know. We'll meet at the picnic tables at Lake Miller. I don't have a copy in my possession right now."

"Why don't I just come by your apartment?"

"Do you want it or not?"

"Okay, okay." He'd play secret agent if that's what it took to get the document. "Who's giving you the report?" He guessed it was Betty Stokes. She'd tipped him and handed over Dwight's phone number.

"A source I cannot reveal," Dwight said. "And let's get one thing straight. I need your word of honor you won't tell anybody where you got it. You'll leave my name out of this story all the way. I'm hoping to get back into police work, and if my name is connected to this story, I'll be blackballed by every police department in North Carolina."

Ronald performed ethical calculus in his head. Dwight made his skin crawl. He'd confessed to being comfortable trying to cover up a crime. But he could provide the accident report; that was the main thing. "Okay," Ronald said, and shook his new source's hand. Then he hurried out, eager to escape the apartment's acrid stench.

He was making his move. In a year or two, he'd be chugging beers with Carl Bernstein. All he had to do was convince Mr. Carlton to stand up to Chief Smithers. He'd be in a stronger position to do that when he had the accident report in hand.

CHAPTER
ELEVEN

The hostess at Pizza Hut led Ronald and Monica to a booth and said, "Is this okay?"

Ronald said, "It's fine," but it wasn't. On the other side of the wall a commode flushed, and a guy said, "Whoa."

Snap prepped him for the date with Monica, last name Timbes. She grew up in Millerton and her dad owned a real estate and insurance agency. She was a brainiac and an artsy type in high school, then went to Hollins College, a girls' school in Virginia, for her undergraduate degree. She didn't come back home much. Snap had no intelligence on her dating history.

After ordering a pepperoni pizza and a salad they clinked glasses—his full of draft beer, hers white wine. The commode flushed again. Ronald cringed and said, "I hope the pizza crust is thicker than these walls." She grinned but didn't laugh. She wore a white peasant blouse edged with flowers and denim bell-bottoms. Her hair was shiny.

"Do you like your job?" she said. "I grew up here, so I know what *The Eagle* is like. I can't imagine working for I.J. Carlton. For a professional communicator, he's terrible at communicating with people."

"The job interview was agonizing. He was more uncomfortable than me." Ronald felt guilty about making his boss look bad, even though Monica was accurate about Mr. Carlton's social awkwardness. "*The Eagle* is in the minor leagues, but I had to start somewhere."

"And your professional goal?"

That sounded like a job interview question. "To move up to a bigger paper."

"Such as?"

"Ultimately *The Washington Post*. Isn't that where every reporter wants to work?"

"Ah," she said. Did that mean "makes sense" or "get real"?

She was working on a doctorate in American literature at the University of Florida and was spending time with her parents before returning to school. Her dissertation was about Flannery O'Connor, one of his least favorite southern authors. She knew everything about O'Connor—had even visited her house in Georgia—and had read everything O'Connor wrote at least twice. She'd read O'Connor's hit story, "Good Country People," a total of twenty-two times. Ronald started to say, "That's kind of excessive," but instead said, "Why do you like it so much?" She blathered in English departmentese for five minutes.

The speak-the-truth life philosophy he adopted a few days earlier was being put to the test and failing. If he came out and told Monica what he thought about Flannery O'Connor, she'd sour on him. Then he'd never have another date with the only person in Millerton he wanted to talk to besides Shelly and Snap.

Their food arrived. Monica ate most of one piece of pizza and a salad. She was slender, and Ronald didn't expect her to be a chowhound. She placed both hands around the wineglass so her fingertips touched in front. Her lips settled into a Mona Lisa half-grin. The other voices in the room faded away.

"I couldn't wait to get out of Millerton," she said. "There's nothing for me here. At least you found one of the few jobs in town with the potential to make a difference. Newspaper reporters are the only thing protecting us from monsters like Richard Nixon."

A fellow Nixon hater. He'd expected as much. A truthful response would be, "I don't slay many monsters. All I do is write cop briefs and stories about poor people who commit crimes." He said to her, "I'm going to make a difference. I'm going to nail a guy named Lamont Moody to the floor." He told her all about the investigation.

"Lamont's your Nixon," she said.

"He's my white whale. He's my green light at the end of Daisy Buchanan's dock, and my scarlet letter. He's the snow on top of Mount Kilimanjaro."

"Thanks for putting it into terms a grad student in literature can grasp. I know Lamont too, and he is a dirtbag. He tried to cheat my father in a real estate transaction. Dad threatened to take him to court and he paid up."

Ronald met Monica's parents when he picked her up at their home at the country club. Her mother had helmet hair and wore a short skirt that showed off her legs. Her dad was lean and tanned and looked like he'd just played eighteen holes. They were much more fashionable than Ronald's folks.

"I used to babysit Lamont's kids when I was in junior high school," Monica said. "His wife is nice, but he gives me the creeps, not that he ever tried anything on me. He was always kind of drunk." She placed her fingertips on his hand. "Don't turn your head to look but Lamont and his wife are sitting on the other side of the dining room right now."

"We'll have to talk to them." He should have known he'd run into Lamont again. He needed to go back to the core lesson from Boy Scouts: Be prepared.

Ronald paid the bill. As they stood to leave the restaurant, a woman his mother's age ambled over with a smile on her face. She and Monica hugged and complimented each other's attractiveness. Monica introduced him to Lucille Moody.

"I just love the articles you write in *The Eagle*," Lucille said. "I read every single word every single day because I want to know what's happening in my hometown. And you tell me. Thank you so much, Ronald."

Lamont sauntered over, white hair falling over his forehead, and held out his arms to Monica. As they embraced, he leered at Ronald. Then he slipped his arm behind Lucille, settling his right hand on her hip bone like it had enjoyed many hours there.

"Are you girls talking about me again?" he said. The women laughed.

"Honey, this is Ronald Truluck, the reporter at *The Eagle*," Lucille said. "He writes those exciting crime stories about bad guys and bank robbers."

"I'm no bank robber," Lamont said, cuing the laugh track again. He explained they'd already met.

"Good to see you again," Ronald said, adopting the polite hypocrisy that greases society. His truth-only philosophy was in tatters.

"The little old Eaglet," Lamont said. "Been reading it all my life. Gives me a chuckle every morning."

The women smiled but didn't laugh. They knew Lamont was being an ass.

Ronald felt like shooting questions at Lamont, but first he needed to get his facts straight.

"Glad you like it so much. Maybe I'll interview you one day."

"Do you cover the city council? I thought that short hippie woman did. Is it Sandra?"

"Shelly. There's a lot we could talk about. Police department funding. Motor vehicles."

"I'll talk to anybody. That's how I make my living—talking. Isn't that right, Lucille?"

"He never shuts his mouth," she said.

Monica and Lucille went to the bathroom together. As Ronald and Lamont waited by the cash register, Lamont volunteered his philosophy of life.

"A man has to take a stand every hour of every day," he said. "The government, the FBI, the CIA, the civil rights activists, and even the newspapers are out there trying to tear down our rights. Your rights too."

"What about Nixon? Should he have quit?" Ronald asked.

"Nixon screwed up. He should never have made those tapes. That was his mistake."

"What about breaking into the Democratic headquarters?"

"Wake up. Everybody does that."

That was a common opinion in Millerton. The cynicism went deep into every social and economic class.

The two couples left the restaurant. The women hugged, the men shook, then the men hugged the women. It felt weird to hug a woman he'd just met. Lamont said, "Come on down to my lot and I'll give you a great deal on a bulldozer."

Ronald and Monica spent the next fifteen minutes stuck inside his car. Lamont bumped a pickup truck while backing up and left his Bonneville running in the middle of the Pizza Hut lot while arguing with the other driver. People leaving the restaurant stopped to watch. The truck owner pointed at his taillight and rubbed his neck. Lamont gestured with both hands. The truck owner picked up a piece of headlight glass and held it up as evidence.

"Fifty bucks," he said.

"I get it," Monica said. "The guy has the bargaining advantage because Lamont's at fault. He thinks Lamont will give him more money if they keep the insurance companies out of it."

Lamont pointed at the headlight. He touched the man's shoulder, like a friend. He touched his own heart, like he was sharing something intimate. He got the man to start smiling, then nodding. Lamont pulled a twenty dollar bill out of his wallet and held it at head level. The man reached across and took the money. They shook hands and drove away, both smiling.

"Lamont does know how to play the game," Monica said. "I hope you get him, but it won't be easy."

They went to see the movie *Death Wish*, about a New Yorker who becomes a murderous vigilante after street punks kill his wife and rape his daughter. Ronald wished he'd picked a romantic comedy instead. After the movie, Ronald asked if she'd like to come to his apartment for a drink. She shook her head no but didn't say she wanted to go home, which Ronald took as silent assent to drive aimlessly around town.

Before the date, Ronald had filled a garbage bag with debris carpeting his car's interior: old newspapers, cigarette packs, soda cans, and fast-food wrappers. He'd gone to the car wash, waited in line with every other emaciated millworker in Millerton, and spray-washed his car. He vacuumed the floorboard and purchased a pine tree-shaped deodorizer that now hung from the rearview mirror. He stretched a new six-inch piece of duct tape over the rip in the dashboard vinyl. The Galaxie had never looked or smelled better.

They crossed the railroad tracks, passed the city limits sign, and left the streetlights behind. Miles of open pastureland lay ahead. He turned on the radio. A fluty intro poured forth, followed by Paul Anka singing "Having My Baby"—a tribute to marriage and parenthood. He turned off the radio.

"Thank you," Monica said. They spent ten minutes trashing the song as the antithesis of rock 'n' roll and the musical buzzkill of the year, if not the decade.

"I'm flashing back to high school, driving around looking for something to do," she said. "I always feel like I'm being pulled back into the past when I come to Millerton."

"Are you hanging out with old friends? Old boyfriends?"

"I'm not dating anybody. Not here, not in Florida. I meant to tell you in the restaurant that I know Bill Jorgensen. He was my English teacher during my senior year in high school."

Millerton was smaller than he imagined. "Was he a good teacher?"

"He was a joke. He assigned us to write about major American poets and I just didn't feel like writing about American poets, so I wrote about a major British poet. John Keats. It was a good paper—by far the best in the class. He gave me a C. We had a huge argument and he threatened to bring me down to a D."

"Maybe you could call him up and ask him to talk to me? If he could describe what happened in the wreck, it would help my story."

"Sorry. He repels me."

They talked politics the rest of the ride. Monica danced in the street the day Nixon resigned. Gerald Ford was a dunce. She foresaw a long period of Democratic nirvana. She said she needed to go home, and he did a U-turn in the middle of a two-lane road and headed back. He drove up the curving paved driveway, parked in front of the three-car garage, and prepared to make an obligatory pass.

"I had fun," Ronald said. She nodded with a lopsided smile. He leaned in half an inch, which could be written off as a mere body twitch if she didn't take the hint. She advanced a quarter of an inch. The mathematics continued until their lips met. She'd snuck a Lifesaver when he wasn't watching, in expectation of the kiss. She twirled her tongue around Ronald's mouth, though it was a repository for three things she hated: beer, cigarettes, and marijuana.

After three minutes of kissing, he escalated and moved his left hand to her right breast. He'd observed it to be on the small side but well-shaped. That shape, he discovered, was an illusion created by the hard fabric of her bra. He pressed his palm there while kissing and making a moaning sound, which she mimicked. Ronald slid his right hand underneath her blouse in back. She leaned forward, making the move easier. He advanced with a three-level strategy: Kissing Monica's mouth with his mouth while fondling her right breast with his left hand and simultaneously unlatching the bra clasp with the fingers of his right hand. But the clasp was difficult. It required two hands. Needing to regroup, Ronald paused the kissing and nuzzled her neck.

"What's that song you're humming?" Monica said.

It was a foreplay moan, not humming, but he said, "'Somebody to Love,' by Jefferson Airplane."

"Hippie band."

"They had some good songs."

He went back for more kissing. He couldn't ask her to turn around so he could unclasp her bra with both hands. That would make it sound like he didn't know what he was doing. Somebody who wore Gloria Steinem glasses shouldn't be wearing a bra. The front porch light flashed on and off twice and Monica pulled back.

"This *does* makes me feel like I'm in high school," she said.

They disentangled. She swiveled the rearview mirror and smoothed her hair. The light over the garage door revealed fine down over her entire face. She moved in for one more kiss, then she was out of the car and scampering up the sidewalk.

CHAPTER
TWELVE

A few days later, Ronald sat on a picnic table at Oral Johnson Memorial Park at Lake Miller. It was a windless day, and he was sweating while looking over a flat plane of brown water. There were no families sitting at a picnic table pulling pieces of fried chicken from a paper bucket. No teenagers sneaking cigarettes. No ducks shitting in the grass. No Dwight.

After forty-five minutes, Ronald ground out his cigarette and stood up. He was halfway to his car when a copper-colored Oldsmobile Cutlass wheeled into the parking lot, sprayed gravel, and parked. Dwight emerged and slammed the driver's door. He wore jeans, cowboy boots, and a white T-shirt.

"Where've you been?" Ronald said. "I've been waiting almost an hour."

"You said one o'clock," Dwight countered. "I'm early."

"We agreed to meet at noon. You're the one who's late."

"I'm here now. Let's get this over with." He strode toward the spot where Ronald had been waiting. They sat on opposite sides of the table facing each other.

"Do you have it?" Ronald said. "The accident report?"

"You want it, don't you? You know it's a big story, don't you? It could make or break your career. You could move on to a bigger paper and make more money and have a good-looking girlfriend."

How did Dwight know what went on inside his head? "Why are you being such a jerk? I'm here. That proves that I want it."

"Well, I don't think you have the backbone to make the story happen. You can't stand up to Chief Smithers or Lamont Moody and I know your boss I.J. Carlton can't. He's caved in to the chief time after time."

The airspace between them crackled. Dwight had shaved his craggy face. He leaned forward to reassert his size advantage.

"I'm not I.J. Carlton," Ronald said. He didn't blink, having practiced staring at himself in the bathroom mirror. Dwight adjusted his haunch, extracted a piece of paper from the back pocket of his jeans, and dropped it on the picnic table.

There it was, Ronald's ticket to *The Washington Post,* a piece of paper eight-and-a-half inches wide and eleven inches long, folded into quarters. It had assumed the damp curvature of Dwight's butt cheek.

"Let's see what we've got here," Ronald said, unfolding the paper with his fingertips and spreading it out on the picnic table. It was a standard North Carolina accident report and aligned with the details Dwight offered in the conversation in his apartment. Ronald ran his eyes down the report, taking in the words printed in block letters in the information boxes. The report was dated at seven minutes after two in the morning of July 31, 1974. Vehicle one, a black 1973 Pontiac Bonneville sedan, traveled westbound, left the roadway, ran into a yard at 304 Archdale Street in Millerton, and struck a concrete birdbath before coming to rest on the edge of the yard. The weather was clear, surface conditions dry. Excessive damage to the front end of the vehicle. The driver was identified as Lamont Vance Moody, date of birth May 27, 1920, a resident of 44 Lee Lane in Millerton. No passengers.

But information was missing. Did Lamont look, act, or smell drunk? Did he slur his words? Was any test given to determine his level of intoxication? In Ronald's quest to take down Lamont, the report was only a starting point.

"This is real?" Ronald said.

"Yes, Ronald Reporter, very real."

Dwight had signed the report in his loopy, look-at-me cursive. He sat at the picnic table, preening. Even as a disgraced, unemployed, dishonest cop, he took pride in authorship of the half-assed accident report.

"Remember, you don't drag my name into this story," Dwight said. "I'm hoping to get another job in law enforcement sooner or later. If I come out calling Chief Smithers a liar, I'll be screwed. He knows police chiefs all over the state."

"Got it," Ronald said. "And you say Lamont had been drinking?"

"Lamont was drunk as a skunk."

That was one of Ronald's favorite clichés: a skunk tilting back a gin bottle, with one hand on a tree trunk to steady himself.

"Who could tell me Lamont was drunk?" Ronald said.

"I could, but you can't use my name. Joe Stoneman took Lamont home so he could, but he won't do it. Lamont won't be ratting himself out. I didn't see Bill Jorgensen. His wife, Sarah Jorgensen, she's a witness. She could tell you how Lamont was slurring his words and stumbling around, but you've already asked her, and she clammed up, didn't she?"

Ronald nodded. His moves were predictable.

"About Joe Stoneman, what's with that guy?" Ronald said. "He pulled me over one night and tried to intimidate me and said I needed to mind my own business, but he didn't mention Lamont."

"Did this happen before or after you started investigating Lamont?"

"This was the day of, about eight hours after I started asking questions."

"That's Lamont's way of telling you to back off," Dwight said, warming to his role as expert commentator. "Joe owes Lamont because Lamont helped Joe get hired with the PD. For all I know, Lamont told him to do it."

"Stoneman scares me."

"Joe's okay. If I was in a jam, I'd want Joe to be my partner. He's a good cop. He doesn't take any crap, but he's got an edge."

"He always looks pissed off."

"Joe came back from Vietnam kind of screwed up in the head. It made him bitter. Things set him off."

"Like what?"

"Anti-war stuff. Political things. Hippies. People who put down the war. People who don't respect veterans."

People like Ronald. He felt simultaneously sympathetic and fearful of Stoneman. If he decided to take out his anger on somebody, Ronald would be the perfect target.

"What made him that way?" Ronald said.

"I can't tell you, Ronald. I'm not a psychologist. He may have had a bad childhood or something, but I think the war did it."

Talking about Stoneman and Vietnam relaxed Dwight. He'd stopped scowling and scanned the lake. Dwight served in Vietnam too, according to Snap and Linda. Ronald considered asking him about the war but decided not to. The unasked question would be, "Did Vietnam screw up your head, Dwight?"

Ronald had a lot of hard work to do, like convincing Martha and Mr. Carlton to accept an accident report from an unofficial source. Or walking into Chief Smithers's office and calling him a liar and then asking him to please provide a comment. This was a grown-up move. Ronald was twenty-two. He didn't know if he could pull it off, but he had to try.

Witnesses would help. He drove back to Archdale Street and walked up the cracked driveway to Bill and Sarah Jorgensen's house. No yellow Vega. A new birdbath had been positioned inside the circle of rocks in the front yard and the tire tracks were only visible if you looked for them. Sarah Jorgensen answered his knock wearing light-blue nursing scrubs.

"Are you ready to talk about Lamont Moody's wreck?" he said.

"You're not a very good listener. We're not talking to you about anything. We've told you that a bunch of times."

"I've learned a lot since we last talked. I know Lamont knocked over your birdbath. I know he said insulting things to you. I know a police officer put him into a patrol car and drove him away. You must be furious."

"You know a lot. You may be a genius."

"I need confirmation of the accident. You could give it to me. This man, Lamont Moody, is putting himself above the law. That's wrong."

"Don't preach to me. I know more than you about what's right and what's wrong in this world."

She had a point. When you're young, it's almost impossible to assert moral, ethical, or intellectual authority over people older than you, which includes almost every adult in the world. He tried a different tactic. "Could I speak to Mr. Jorgensen?"

"Bill's at work and he wouldn't talk to you anyway."

"Where does he work?"

She shut the door in his face.

CHAPTER THIRTEEN

Ronald called Monica to tell her about his progress on Lamontgate.

"Fabulous," she said. "I'd like to hear more. Why don't you come over to my house when you get off work? My parents went to the beach for a few days, so it's just me."

Millerton was no longer a dirty mill town. It was a beautiful metropolis, full of hope and sunshine and possibly sex. He went home, cleaned up, and smoked a joint in the bathroom. Because there would be no smoking of any kind at her house.

Ronald was not a Romeo. He'd never had a girlfriend, except for a half dozen dates and a couple of drunken dorm couplings with Beth Medford. They met in a college feature writing class. The professor assigned students to interview each other and write profiles. Since they'd already gotten to know each other, asking her out was easy. She was an army brat from a big family and worked as a copy editor for the campus newspaper. She dumped him at Hector's Hot Dog Emporium right before Christmas break, saying she needed to concentrate more on her copy editing.

When he stepped out of the apartment house front door, a neighbor was sitting on the front steps smoking. He was the only one who talked to Ronald. His name was Ronnie and he acted like they had something in common because of their first names.

"Where you going to, buddy?"

"Out to see a friend."

"Is she good looking?"

"How do you know it's a she?"

"Because you're all dressed up."

Ronald had taken a bath, washed his hair, shaved, and put on his Bob Dylan T-shirt. In Ronald's world, that qualified as dressing up. He calculated a rock poet like Dylan would appeal to Monica's literary leanings.

"She is good looking," Ronald said.

"Good luck," Ronnie said. He ground a cigarette butt into the concrete step with his shoe. Ronnie didn't have a car. He walked to his job at the mill. In his mind, Ronald lived like a prince.

When Ronald got to Monica's house, she said "Hey," stretching out the word, and led him through the foyer and into a shining kitchen. She wore a white sleeveless blouse and smelled like soap and shampoo. She pulled a bottle of white wine out of the refrigerator and filled two glasses waiting on the counter. He wanted a beer but didn't say so. They stood in the kitchen, sipping and staring at each other.

They had sex in her queen-sized bed beneath a framed poster of the Beatles during their moptop, pre-acid days. He fought the urge to explain you don't frame a poster—even a Beatles poster that would become a valuable antique in fifty years—you thumbtack the thing to the wall. But it was too early in the relationship to criticize her decorating taste, so he concentrated on the sex.

"Nice room," Ronald said when it was over. The color scheme was pale green and tan, from the wallpaper to the carpet. The furniture matched. He was smothered by good taste.

"My mom did most of it when I was in high school. I'm tired of it now, but I don't live here all the time so I can't complain."

Monica rested her head on his chest. He stroked her hair. She cleared her throat. He repositioned their bodies so they were face-to-face. He was going to say something flattering, after which they'd have sex again, but skipped the conversation and went straight to the sex. Afterward, Ronald described getting the accident report and being rebuffed by Sarah Jorgensen.

"What I heard," Monica said, walking her fingers up his chest, "is they married on the rebound. Bill met his first wife in college. She got tired of him and went to Texas to be with her high school boyfriend. She took the kids, and he was high and dry. Sarah had been married to a construction foreman who was a real jerk. He hit her. Then he got killed in an accident on the job. They didn't have any kids and she was left high and dry too. Bill and Sarah met at church, and they got married. She's working class and he's not, or at least he doesn't think he is. It's a case of opposites attract. That happens a lot, you know."

She breathed into his face, like she was sending a message. Were they opposites? He thought they had a lot in common. Hating Nixon, hating Millerton, having sex.

"Bill wants to talk to me," Ronald said. "If I could get their eyewitness account, my story would be great. It's something the story needs."

"Are you asking me again to ask Bill to talk to you?"

"Kind of. It would help."

She went to the bathroom and returned smelling of toothpaste. They picked their clothes off the floor and dressed on opposite sides of the bed, snickering like co-conspirators. Monica dressed with amazing efficiency and was clothed and combing her hair at the dressing table before Ronald put his socks on. She took Ronald's hand and walked him to the door. They smooched in the foyer and agreed to meet again before she sent him out with a gentle shove to the butt. Ronald lit a cigarette in the Galaxie and drove away, singing along with a used car lot commercial.

As he turned onto the street where his apartment was located, a patrol car behind him hit the lights, but not the siren. Ronald recognized the approaching bulk in the rear view mirror. Joe Stoneman. Ronald was glad he'd only drunk two glasses of wine and didn't have any marijuana in the car. He rolled down the window and said, "Hello, Joe."

Stoneman wasn't having any chitchat. "Do you remember the last time we talked?" he said. "It was a situation just like this, on a dark street."

"I do remember. We had a very pleasant conversation."

Sex made Ronald confident to a dangerous degree. If he was beaten to a pulp, it would be Monica's fault.

"I said you needed to fix your attitude," Stoneman said. "You haven't done that."

"You were unspecific."

"Get out of the car." Standing, their size difference was accentuated. Stoneman even smelled big. He put his hand on Ronald's chest and pushed him back against his car. "I know what you're trying to do. You're stirring up trouble. You need to learn your place. Let the police do the investigating, and then you can write your stories."

"Did Lamont tell you to pull me over?"

Cops didn't like to answer questions, but Ronald kept asking them. It was a particular mental illness that affected reporters.

"You're still living in that dumpy house with those drunks," Stoneman said. "I gave you some good advice last time. You need to consider moving. Like, to another town."

Stoneman drove away and Ronald went home. He didn't even try to sleep. His fear of being killed by Joe Stoneman was counterbalanced by exhilaration. The threats proved Ronald was on the right track.

CHAPTER FOURTEEN

"It looks like it's been through the washing machine," Martha said.

Ronald hadn't done a good job of taking care of the accident report. He shouldn't have folded it into eighths and thrust it into the breast pocket of his shirt when he left the picnic tables. The report had frayed at the edges and ripped at two of the folds. Some words were blurry. "Bonneville" was illegible unless you knew what you were looking for, but the name "Lamont Vance Moody" was clear.

"What do you think?" Martha said to Mr. Carlton. "Can we go with it?"

I.J. Carlton was incapable of making a snap decision. He exhaled and stood. He put his hands in his pockets and walked the perimeter of the newsroom, pausing to read a sports story thumbtacked to the wall behind Snap's desk. Martha slid her cardigan sweater sleeves up to her elbows. Ronald leaned against the desk and studied the framed photo of Mr. Carlton and his son holding up fish at a lake. Mr. Carlton sat down again. He positioned his chin on his fists and studied the accident report again. He removed his glasses.

"So you've been working on this story behind my back?" the editor said. "I thought you were going to tell us what you were up to."

"I've done it on my own time. It hasn't cut into the routine police coverage. It's an important story."

"Well," the editor said. He said "well" a lot, with varying intonations. He was the John Coltrane of "well." He settled back into his chair and sighed. Martha sighed. Ronald decided he might as well sigh.

"It looks like the real thing. And you're saying Dwight Bennett wrote this accident report and gave it to you?" Ronald explained he'd gotten it by promising Dwight anonymity. Mr. Carlton shook his head. "You're pushing it. You know my rule about unnamed sources."

"I guess you heard why Dwight was fired." Ronald told him the official reason and the real reason—Dwight's affair with Stick's daughter.

"I believe it," Mr. Carlton cackled and began packing a pipe. Having a new reason to trash Stick took his attention away from Ronald's unauthorized reporting. "She's been exposed to a bad role model in her father. Stick doesn't have a lick of morals or brains or anything."

"I thought Cynthia had more sense than that," Martha said. She cast an admiring eye at Ronald. He'd scored crucial local gossip ahead of her and earned partial forgiveness for his sins. He told them about being pushed around by Joe Stoneman the night before.

"He got physical with you?" Mr. Carlton said. "Were you giving him any lip?"

"A little, but nothing to warrant being shoved against the car," Ronald said. "He said we need to leave the investigating to the police."

"He said that?" Mr. Carlton laced his fingers together while keeping the pipe clamped between his teeth. He needed to do something to save face—or at least act like he was doing something for the sake of appearances. He'd never stood up to the police chief before. Ronald was forcing the issue.

"That's why it's time for me to talk to Lamont," Ronald said.

It took half an hour for Mr. Carlton to convince himself he needed to bend the rules. Everybody knew about the wreck, but Ronald had proven an accident report really existed. That was enough reason to ask some questions. And Lamont was enough of a loose cannon that he might come out and admit he had the wreck.

"I'm not saying we'll run the story," Mr. Carlton said. "You're just asking questions because it's in the public interest. Stick to the facts."

Ronald set up the interview with Lamont at three o'clock at his heavy equipment business. Then he went to McDonald's with Shelly to discuss strategy.

"You've typed up questions on a piece of paper in fourteen-point type, right?" she said.

"Why would I do that?" Ronald said.

"Because you'll be nervous at the interview. You don't want to think up questions on the spot. It's what Steve does for a big interview."

Ronald pushed his tray to the side. He couldn't eat; he was nervous. "I'll ask, 'How drunk were you? Did you bribe the cops?'"

"Too obvious," Shelly said. "I'll be right back."

Ronald thought she was going to the bathroom, but Shelly walked out of McDonald's and into the Esso gas station next door. Ronald wrote questions on a napkin, starting with, "Where were you the night of July thirty-first?" but scratched it out because he didn't want to sound like a TV cop. Shelly returned.

"I called Steve at his office. I didn't have enough dimes for the pay phone so I bought a Mounds bar to get some change." She put the candy bar on the table; she was on a diet, though that hadn't stopped her from ordering a Big Mac. "He said to ask questions based on the accident report and catch Lamont in a lie. For instance, what kind of car did he wreck?"

"A 1973 Bonneville sedan."

"You should ask, 'When and where did you wreck the Bonneville?' And if Mr. Lamont Moody says he doesn't know what you're talking about, you reach into your briefcase and bring out the accident report and slap it down on his desk."

"I don't have a briefcase."

"Then you drill into him. How many beers did you drink that night? If he says I didn't drink anything, you say, 'A witness at the scene told me the floor of your car was carpeted —carpeted!—in empty beer cans. And Officer

Bennett says you stank of liquor and couldn't stand up straight. And he says another police officer arrived on the scene and took you home in a patrol car, thus allowing you to avoid justice."

"I told Dwight I wouldn't use his name," Ronald said. "What if Lamont says, 'Where did you get the accident report?'"

"Say it's a source you cannot name," Shelly said. "That stops them every time."

CHAPTER FIFTEEN

Lamont ran Moody's Heavy Equipment Company out of a brick house on the bypass that used to be a family home. It still had a sloped roof with a chimney and a front porch with a wooden railing. The building was surrounded by hulking pieces of equipment, like bulldozers, backhoes, and graders. Ronald drove through the open gate of a chain-link fence topped with barbed wire, feeling like he'd entered a minimum-security prison. He parked between a dust-covered Bonneville and a Chevy Impala. Inside, a woman with a baked-in frown sat behind a cheap desk in what used to be the living room. She stood, opened a wooden door, and said, "He's here." Ronald walked through the door in attack mode.

Lamont's personal office occupied what used to be the main bedroom of the house. The man himself sat behind a desk in a high-backed leather office chair, looking composed in a button-down dress shirt with a tie, but the rest of his office was a jumble. Boxes of machine parts were stacked as high as Ronald's waist along with piles of gears and sprockets. Tires leaned against a wall. A motorcycle had been taken apart on an oil-spotted blanket.

Ronald stepped over a lawnmower and reached Lamont's desk. The whole room smelled like gasoline.

"It's good to see you, Mr. Moody," Ronald said.

"What's so good about it?"

"Because I've been wanting to talk to you about something."

"Then let's talk. I've got things to do."

Ronald moved a heavy cardboard box off a chair. It clinked.

"Beer mugs. Somebody got them from a restaurant going out of business and gave me the box as a present. I don't need any beer mugs but didn't want to hurt the guy's feelings, so I took 'em. You want 'em? You can have the whole damn box."

A commode flushed. A door Ronald hadn't noticed opened and a man in blue work clothes walked out buckling his pants and wheezing, a cloud of internal body odors rolling behind him.

"Feel better?" Lamont said.

"Ten pounds lighter," the man said. He was big and rotund but not soft.

"This is Turkey Stoneman. He repairs the machines on my lot and then some," Lamont said. "The man's a genius. Turkey, this is Mr. Ronald Truluck from *The Eagle*. He's here to write a big story about me."

"For doing what?" Turkey said. "Getting drunk? That ain't news."

"Are you related to Joe Stoneman with the police department?" Ronald said.

"Brother."

That meant two big guys were looking out for Lamont. Turkey extended a right hand that moments earlier had explored his nether regions. If Ronald shook, he might be contaminated by Turkey's bacteria. To not shake would cast a pall over the interview. Ronald made a professional sacrifice.

Turkey started working on the motorcycle. Ronald looked at Lamont to let him know he was supposed to ask Turkey to leave the room because the questioning was going to get intense, so intense he might lose the respect of his employee. Lamont opened his palms.

"Do you always drive Bonnevilles?" Ronald said.

"Hell, I've driven ten Bonnevilles. I've been driving Bonnevilles since they started making them. Good car. Which one are you talking about?"

"I'm interested in the one you wrecked."

"I've wrecked at least two Bonnevilles, and my son wrecked the other one."

Lamont and Turkey reminisced about their legendary car wrecks. They never just ran into a ditch. Every car flipped over twenty times, exploded in flames, went airborne, was impaled on a guardrail, or was cut in half by a speeding freight train after stalling out on railroad tracks.

"How about the Bonneville you ran into the birdbath in the front yard at 304 Archdale Street during the early morning hours of July 31, 1974?" Ronald asked.

"Let me think." Lamont stroked his mustache. "I'm not sure I was involved in such an accident. Turkey, does that strike a chord with you?"

Turkey walked to the desk. "Nope," he said.

"It happened," Ronald said.

"He said he don't remember," Turkey said.

"Lamont said he wasn't sure if he was involved in such a wreck, which is different from not remembering," Ronald said.

"Don't be putting words in this man's mouth," said Turkey, not a fan of semantics. "He's a good man, an honest man. He does not lie or steal. You understand me?"

Ronald wished he had a briefcase, so he could hide the pistol he might need in case Turkey attacked.

"If the wreck didn't happen, how can you explain this?" Ronald said. He withdrew the accident report from his manila folder and slapped it on top of the mess of invoices, used napkins, and newspapers spread across Lamont's desktop.

"What's that?" Turkey said.

"It's the accident report from that wreck," Ronald said.

"This thing is not real," Lamont said, holding the report close to his face. "This is not an official, certified police accident report. It's meaningless." He tossed the paper onto his desk.

"An investigating police officer wrote the report," Ronald said. "I talked to the officer. He says you were intoxicated."

"Dwight Bennett?" Lamont said. "He's a scoundrel! You can't believe a word he says. The chief fired him."

"I'm not identifying the officer. I swore to keep his name out of this, and I'll never, ever tell anybody," Ronald said. "I'll go to jail before I reveal the officer's name. But why are you saying it was Dwight Bennett? How did you happen to pluck his name out of the air? Because you saw him at the scene the night when you wrecked your car, didn't you?"

"Because his name is right here on the bottom of the accident report," Lamont said.

Ronald forgot about Dwight's signature. That made anonymous sourcing pointless. But Ronald made a promise and he had to stick with it until Dwight released him from it.

"I cannot identify my source," he said.

"Why the hell not?"

"Because I gave my word of honor."

Lamont chuckled from deep in his throat. "You've got more honor than brains."

"Never mind that. Do you deny wrecking your Bonneville on Archdale Street?" Ronald said.

"I'm not saying I didn't have a wreck, and I'm not saying I did have a wreck. I'm saying you don't have any proof one way or the other."

"That makes sense to me," Turkey said.

"This accident report is proof, whether you like it or not," Ronald said. "And I have more. My source told me there were beer cans all over the floor of your car and you had trouble standing up. I know everything that happened."

"Dwight told you that?"

"I'm not saying it's Dwight."

"You're not saying a lot of things," Lamont said.

Turkey went back to the motorcycle. Lamont opened the desk drawer and pulled out a big business checkbook. Was he going to offer a monetary bribe to back off the story? Ronald swelled with outrage—and curiosity about how much he'd be offered. Five hundred dollars seemed about right.

"Tell you what," Lamont said. "I'll pay the city for towing the car, how about that? How much does it come to?"

Ronald and Lamont both sat with pens poised, ready to write something.

"So, now you're saying the wreck happened?" Ronald said.

"I'm saying it's in the police department's discretion about how to handle this situation, if it happened, which I'm not saying it did. And looky here, Ronald, there's no breath test or anything on this accident report, so how could I be drunk?"

"I don't know about that, Lamont," Turkey said, "because one time I wrecked my truck on Tubman Road and the deputy just took me home because I didn't hurt anybody. It was a one-vehicle wreck. They didn't give me a breath test but if they did it would've said, 'Turkey is shit-faced.'"

"Never mind, Turkey. Would you mind going to my car and seeing if I left my reading glasses out there?"

"Well, hell," Turkey said. "If you didn't want me here, why'd you ask me to stick around in the first place?" He left the room.

"So how much?" Lamont said.

"I don't want you to write a check. I just want you to give me straight answers."

"I've answered your questions."

"You've spewed bullshit."

"You're trying to trick me into saying something incriminating," Lamont said, pointing at Ronald with his ballpoint pen. "You're a lot smarter than you look."

It was obvious flattery, but it still felt good. Lamont slid open his desk drawer again and withdrew a package of Winston cigarettes. He shook one out, lit up, and laid the package on the edge of the desk. He was inviting Ronald to bum a smoke—the first step in a seduction. Smoke flowed out of Lamont's nostrils and kissing-shaped lips. Ronald stayed strong.

"Let's get down to brass tacks," Lamont said. "Why do you hate me? You don't really know me. What have I done to make you so angry?"

Ronald had run into this attitude before, over and over. People in Millerton didn't ignore the principles of good governance or good journalism. They didn't know they existed. Everything was personal.

"I don't hate you," Ronald said. "But you broke the law and got away with it just because you're on the city council. That's not right. Everybody should be equal in the eyes of the law."

"Of course," Lamont said. "This is the United States of America. And because I live in the US of A, I don't have to tell you anything. You've got nothing on me except for a fake accident report from a lying dirtbag."

Lamont rocked back and forth in his chair, a bully's smile plastered across his jowly, lined face. Ronald had lost control of the interview. "Why did you change your position on the new police station?" he said

Lamont didn't flinch. "I don't have to explain myself to you."

"I represent the public. I think you do."

Lamont exhaled, sending a small cloud of smoke over Ronald's head. "I'm through talking to you."

Ronald collected his notebook and papers while Lamont observed him with narrowed eyes. With Lamont's offer to write a check, he'd gotten a halfway confession. The receptionist pushed him out the door with her eyes. Outside, Turkey sat in a bulldozer cab scowling as Ronald drove away.

CHAPTER SIXTEEN

Ronald needed to warn Dwight face-to-face that the cover had been blown. It was the honorable and ethical thing to do.

Nobody answered his knock at Dwight's apartment, so Ronald drove to Dwight's mother's house on Table Street. Linda from the office said he could be found there at times. It turned out to be Millerton's top tourist attraction. Dwight's mother had assembled possibly the largest private collection of yard statuary to occupy a personal residence in North Carolina, according to the story written by Anne, the women's page editor. Anne framed the story and it hung on the wall behind her desk.

At any time, a rotating cast of at least forty small statues would be arranged in the front yard. The usual gnomes and jockey boys, but also maidens holding bowls of fruit, a wolf painted blue, four birdbaths, a two-foot-tall pineapple painted red, a lighthouse, and a replica of Michelangelo's David with a napkin tied around his waist to hide his genitals. Dwight's mother's brother and a cousin were truck drivers and brought her a new statue every time they went out of state.

Ronald tapped on the storm door and stepped back two paces. Sometimes people wouldn't open it if you stood too close. A wrinkled woman opened the door wearing a rust-red McDonald's uniform. Just looking at her outfit of pure polyester made Ronald itch. He introduced himself.

"I guess you want to write another story about my yard," she said. "I didn't know you were coming. I got two hours before I start my next job."

"You've got two jobs?"

"I got three jobs. I clean houses for people, and I take in ironing, too."

She walked into the yard and placed a hand on a concrete lion's head.

"This one came from San Francisco, California." She tapped a pirate. "He's from New Orleans. I've never been there. I've just been outside North Carolina once in my entire life, and that was when I went on my honeymoon to Myrtle Beach, South Carolina. Ever been there?"

He had. One spring break, Ronald became separated from his friends in the crowd on Ocean Boulevard. He couldn't remember the name of their motel, so he slept on a bench until the cops rousted him at four in the morning. He wandered around until reconnecting with his friends by chance. Spring break, like most college traditions, was overrated.

"I'm not here to write about your statues. I'm looking for Dwight. Somebody told me he might be here."

She inspected Ronald with a cool intensity, her eyes lingering on his ankle-high work boots. He'd never worn them while performing actual manual labor. She picked up a piece of white paper that had blown into her yard and slid it into her uniform pocket.

"If he wants to get hold of you, he will. Dwight's a grown man. He pays his taxes and takes care of his child. He respects his mother. He served his country."

"I'm glad he made it back from Vietnam. We lost too many good men there."

Again, she gave him the cold eyeball. "You didn't serve, did you? You don't have the look."

"I didn't have the opportunity."

"You couldn't enlist? Were you 4-F? Is there something wrong with you?"

"I just didn't have to go."

"You're one of the lucky ones."

She climbed the steps onto the porch. The deadbolt snapped into place like a gunshot.

CHAPTER SEVENTEEN

Ronald drove five miles down Tar Pit Road, looking for the antenna-less red Malibu that Linda Lasseter described. When a mail truck passed him going in the other direction, Ronald did a U-turn and the mailman gave him the address for Teresa Tyler Bennett, Dwight's ex-wife.

She lived in a double-wide trailer mounted on cinder blocks that was plopped in the middle of a treeless, newly cut acre of grass. The Malibu was parked on the side of the trailer with its hood up, unseeable from the road. A gleaming Ford pickup was parked in front along with a John Deere riding lawnmower that emanated the narcotic smell of just-cut grass and gasoline. Somebody was home.

Ronald turned off his car and waited. Two dogs, a terrier and a long brown hound, slid from under the trailer and began barking and moving in tandem. The hound placed his front paws on the Galaxie hood and stared at Ronald like he was fresh meat. The trailer's front door swung open and a lean headneck stepped onto the wooden porch.

"Boogie! Ricky!" the man yelled. "Get the hell away from that car."

The dogs retreated but didn't go far, circling like sharks in the water. Ronald stepped out of the Galaxie but kept the door open in case he had to jump back inside.

"I'm lookin' for a lady by the name of Teresa Tyler Bennett. If she live here, I'm needin' to talk with her." Bad grammar put the lower classes at ease.

"Hey, T," the man yelled, not taking his eyes off Ronald. "Some guy's here to see you."

Dwight's ex stepped to the front door and whispered to the man about thirty seconds before coming down the stairs and taking a position on the other side of Ronald's car.

"I'm Teresa Tyler," she said, "and who the hell are you?" With lank hair and tired eyes, she looked like she spent too much time inside the trailer watching TV.

"I'm a friend of your ex-husband," Ronald said. That was the wrong thing to say.

"If you're Dwight's buddy, you can get the hell out of here."

Her companion came off the porch and stood next to her. He was wiry with well-defined forearm muscles. He looked curious, not angry, but he might turn out to be the kind of guy who went from calm to homicidal in five seconds.

"I'm a reporter for *The Eagle*," Ronald said. "I need to tell Dwight something. Somebody told me he's here sometimes."

"Are you crazy?" Teresa said. "I won't let him on this property. Tell him that, Troy, tell him what I said last time Dwight came around."

"You said, 'I'll kill you, you son of a bitch,'" Troy said. "And I said, 'You won't have to, Teresa, because I'm going to kill him first.' And you said, 'Don't deny me that pleasure.' And I said, 'Let's flip a coin.' And you said, 'I'm going to shoot his ass.' And I said, 'Don't waste a bullet because I'll strangle Dwight with my bare hands. I don't care if he is a cop.'"

Troy flexed his fingers to demonstrate his strangling technique. Teresa looked skyward and said, "Dwight, you jerk."

"I guess you haven't heard about Dwight," Ronald said.

"I heard he's a lying bastard who'd screw a mailbox," Troy said.

"Dwight's not working for the police department now."

That was the right thing to say. Teresa and Troy became attentive.

"What happened?" Teresa asked. "Was he stealing money from the petty cash drawer again?"

"He says the police chief didn't like him," Ronald said.

"Nobody likes Dwight. I'll bet he took marijuana out of the evidence room and smoked it with high school girls after football games. He's done that before. Sometimes he drank on the job. And somebody told me he was having sex with the mayor's daughter in the back seat of his patrol car in the police department parking lot. Did he get her pregnant?"

She'd just given Ronald several story leads. He wouldn't pursue any of them until Lamontgate played out. Then Dwight would be expendable.

"I'll ask Dwight about that," Ronald said. "Where could I find him?"

"He could be anywhere," Teresa said. "Sleeping in a ditch, at a massage parlor, or in that expensive apartment he lives in."

Troy wrapped his arm around her shoulder and they leaned into each other.

"Dwight sure turned into an asshole," Troy said. "He used to be a pretty good guy."

"What happened? Some people say Vietnam messed up Dwight's head," Ronald said.

"I don't see why that would've happened, since he drove a supply truck," Troy said. "He didn't do any fighting. If he told you that, he's lying. He never saw one second of combat."

"Are you certain?" Ronald said. "I mean, this is a serious accusation. Do you have copies of his military records?"

"Records?" Troy said.

"I don't have any military records, but I think I know what happened," Teresa said, exasperated. "People wanted to make Dwight some kind of war hero and he let them. He didn't exactly lie, but he never corrected anybody either." She shrugged. "It did help him get hired at the police department, so I don't blame him. And now he's gone and gotten fired."

The dogs sniffed Ronald's feet. Teresa said she made jewelry and sold it at flea markets. She went inside the trailer to get a business card in case

Ronald ever needed to buy earrings for his girlfriend's birthday. Troy exuded calm. Ronald asked what was wrong with the Malibu and Troy said, "Valves." Ronald nodded like he understood. Teresa returned with a young girl in her arms and handed Ronald the business card. If he ever needed to hunt down Dwight again, he could call instead of driving out to the trailer.

"Will you give Dwight a message?" Teresa said. "Would you tell him I need my child support? We can work out something on what he owes. We're tired of having to depend on my mother to buy Amber new panties because she's outgrown the old ones. Will you tell him that?"

Dwight was more dishonest than Ronald imagined. Besides leaving crucial information off the Lamont Moody accident report and not coming clean about why he got fired, Dwight didn't even pay his child support. He might have lied about Vietnam—or let people get the wrong idea. Though Ronald hated the Vietnam war in general and the ROTC guys on campus in particular, he still harbored a secret idealism about the American military. That attitude came from watching too many World War II television shows, like *Combat* and *The Rat Patrol*. The overarching message: Soldiers in combat were closer than biological brothers. If Dwight would violate that sacred bond, he would lie about the accident report being real.

Ronald went back to Paradise Apartments and found Dwight at home watching a cop show on TV. He described the interview with Lamont.

"I forgot I signed it," Dwight said. "Now everybody will know I'm your source. This could screw up everything."

"There's more. Lamont says the report's a fake and I'm wondering the same thing. I need confirmation the report is the real thing."

He didn't tell Dwight why he was suddenly skeptical.

CHAPTER EIGHTEEN

The interior of Dwight's Cutlass was spotless—no soda cans or crumbs—and it smelled like leather and saddle soap. A few miles outside the city limits, he turned at a massive mailbox and the Cutlass crawled down a smooth dirt driveway for a hundred yards to a two-story farmhouse. A woman opened the door. Ronald knew her from somewhere. She was in her forties with a broad face and wore a floral muumuu. "You guys come in," she said.

It was Betty Stokes, the Millerton police desk sergeant. Ronald knew her as a neutered creature in an ill-fitting cop uniform with chemical warfare breath. In her home, Betty looked, smelled, and moved like a woman. Not somebody Ronald wanted to sleep with, because she was too old, but a member of that team. Ronald was surprised somebody in Millerton was smart enough to pull off a double life. He had assumed Betty lived in a one-bedroom apartment and ate TV dinners with her cat. Keeping police reports in proper alphabetical order was her only joy in life.

She and Dwight parked him in a formal living room. Ronald sat on a lumpy sofa. The room was filled with antiques, like the porcelain figurines of Japanese samurai arranged on top of a dark wooden coffee table.

From the kitchen came the sound of melodramatic music, the ten thousand violins of Mantovani, Ronald's mother's favorite zone-out music after a hard day. A voice from the kitchen joined the surging crescendo of emotion. It was Betty, singing, like he wasn't sitting there judging her furniture. Dwight walked out and returned carrying a tray holding three cans of Budweiser beer. Betty followed with frosted mugs, like you'd find at a fancy restaurant. Everybody poured their beers.

"I hear you had a conversation with our friend Lamont today," she said. She chuckled when Ronald told her about Lamont's offer to write a check. "Now, what is it you wanted to ask me?"

"I guess Dwight filled you in on what I'm looking for. Did you give him the accident report?"

"Are we off the record?" After Ronald nodded, she said, "I did."

"I thought so. That's good to know because I had to make sure it was authentic. Why are you doing it, Betty? You have a lot to lose, like your job."

"Before I tell you, let me ask you a question," Betty said. "Why do you hate Lamont? What has he done to you?"

"I don't hate Lamont," Ronald said. "He was driving drunk and the police didn't arrest him because he's on the city council. Under the law, everyone should be treated as an equal. It's nothing personal."

Betty put down her mug and held a napkin to her lips.

"Nothing personal?" she said. "Are you crazy? Everything is personal. If you don't hate Lamont with all your heart, well then, I don't know if I should trust you."

"I *don't* hate Lamont," Ronald said. "I'm neutral. Unbiased."

Betty whooped and convulsed with coughs. Dwight laughed too. He walked out and returned with a package of Salems and a red Zippo lighter. Betty lit a cigarette and settled back into her corner of the sofa.

"You're killing me," Betty said. "Nobody's neutral in this world, including you, though you may not know it. Let me explain. I'm not doing this because I'm trying to stamp out corruption. There will always be corruption, no matter who's in charge. Corruption is a byproduct of bureaucratic competence."

Betty wasn't just a paper pusher. She had a philosophy. Her cynicism went deeper than Ronald imagined.

"I'm helping you," she said, "because I hate Ellen Swicegood."

He also hated the gangster of city hall. He could see bending his principles to hurt her. Maybe Betty was onto something.

"I thought you two got along," he said. "I've seen you chatting with her by the Coke machine. Was that a charade?"

"I'm putting up a front. Ellen is trying to screw me."

"This is bad," Dwight said. "It's so typical."

Betty lit a new cigarette with the last of a burning butt. "Once a month, I tally all the incident reports by category, plus the accident reports, and deliver them in a folder to Ellen. She counts them again for the monthly report for the chief, like I'm incapable of doing it myself. She just copies my numbers.

"But I compared Ellen's totals for July to mine and she came up with one less accident report. That's Lamont's wreck. When I asked her about it, she had the gall to sit there behind her big desk and say I added up the numbers wrong. Ellen didn't know I've been making copies of all the reports for my own private file for the last few months, just in case."

She chuckled at her cleverness.

"I showed her my copies and proved her wrong. She blew a gasket, but I stood my ground. I mentioned the problem to Chief Smithers and he said he'd talk to Ellen. But since then he's been very cold to me, and she's been an absolute bitch. She's been losing accident reports to cover for people like Lamont. And now that they know I'm onto their game, the chief wants to take me off the front desk and make me a school crossing guard or something. Me! After twenty years. I'm not putting up with it. I'll quit. I'll go out in a blaze of glory."

"Damn straight," Dwight said.

They rode in silence back to Paradise Apartments. Betty and Dwight were just like Lamont. All conflict was reduced to personal grudges. Nobody even thought about principles or abstractions. The world was one big pissing match, so you might as well unzip and go for it. Ronald promised himself to never become like them, but a troubling thought tickled his brain. What if they were right about the way the world worked, and he was wrong?

Dwight parked and turned off the engine.

"Listen, I was looking for you earlier today and went to Teresa and Troy's trailer, thinking you might be there," Ronald said. "They said you broke quite a few rules when you worked for the police, like having sex with Cynthia in the police department parking lot. Did you?"

"You talked to my ex? Are you kidding? Are you investigating me or Lamont Moody?"

Dwight got out of the car and sped up the steps to his apartment. He was putting the key into the deadbolt when Ronald caught up to him.

"I always scrutinize my sources when I grant them anonymity," Ronald said. He prayed Dwight didn't read the paper and wouldn't know he'd never used an anonymous source.

"It's your story but it's my life," Dwight yelled. Ronald followed him into the apartment. Dwight paced. "If the story goes bad, nothing will happen to you, but I'll be blackballed from policing for the rest of my life, maybe worse. I'm not going to work as a damn security guard." He paced some more. "I know you're gullible, Ronald, so let me say it in plain English: Teresa is the biggest liar in Miller County. She's bitter."

Dwight started trashing his ex-wife and wouldn't stop, so Ronald left. When he reached the parking lot, Dwight came out on the balcony and yelled, "And leave my name out of this story. You promised me you'd do that. Keep your word for a change."

"Everybody knows. What's the point?"

"Keep your promise!" Dwight said and went back inside.

Ronald was still worried about using Dwight's accident report, despite Betty's assurance it was real. If Dwight lied about his military service and people found out he was the source for Lamontgate, Ronald's story would be tainted, no matter how solid the reporting. Ronald needed to find out about Dwight and Vietnam. He needed Dwight's military records.

When he got to his apartment, Ronald called Shelly's house, knowing she was covering a night meeting. Steve answered. He segued into a long story about his days as a helicopter door gunner in Vietnam before answering Ronald's question.

"You'll need to write to the National Personnel Records Center in St. Louis to get this guy's military records. But it will take a long time if it can be done at all. There was a fire last year and a lot of paperwork on people who served in the army burned up. The fire screwed up the whole records retrieval system."

Ronald heard ice cubes clinking on the other end of the line. He went to the refrigerator and got a beer. They were two reporters drinking and talking shop. Steve told a meandering tale about covering a broom factory fire on a winter night. After twenty minutes he dispensed his advice: Keep a pencil handy because ballpoint pens will freeze up in below-freezing weather. Shelly came home from her meeting complaining about the idiocy of the Miller County Board of Commissioners. Steve needed to go to the bathroom and handed her the phone. She and Ronald talked about Mr. Carlton's eyepatch and made fun of Linda Lasseter's hair and Anne's perfume. When they hung up, Ronald looked at his clock. He'd talked on the phone for three hours.

CHAPTER NINETEEN

Ronald arrived fifteen minutes early for the interview in Chief Smithers' office. Ellen Swicegood was reading the newspaper. She ignored Ronald, like he was a panhandler who wandered into the office.

"I have an appointment with the chief," he said. "Could you tell him I've arrived?"

Ronald should have said, "Tell him I've arrived" as an order, rather than the question that came out of his mouth and put him in a subservient position. She sat unmoving, a newspaper page pressed between her thumb and forefinger.

"Have a seat," she said.

Ronald took a chair against the wall. A well-used Bible lay on her desk for easy reference in case she needed to condemn him to hell with scripture. At five minutes before nine, Arthur Fleetwood Sr., the city attorney for Millerton, sauntered into the waiting room wearing a dark business suit and a very white shirt. He didn't say hello to Ronald. Ellen let him into the chief's private office.

Ronald was about to be double-teamed—triple-teamed if you counted Ellen. His weapons were the accident report and a list of questions he'd jotted down that morning while drinking instant coffee and smoking a joint to calm down. The opposition was armed with the power of arrest, a law degree, and a secretary with laser vision that could sterilize a man at one hundred yards.

Ellen finished the paper, folded it into quarters, and dropped it into her wastebasket. She left the office and returned with coffee. At 9:30, Ronald approached her desk.

"What's the problem?" he said. "I had an appointment to see the chief at 9:00."

"There's no problem." She didn't even look up.

"He's thirty minutes late."

"That's not a problem for me. Not for the chief."

"I've got things to do." He had nothing except his cop rounds. "If Chief Smithers doesn't want to see me, he should have said so."

Now she looked up. Without moving her eyes, she reached for her phone, lifted the receiver, and pushed a button. "Ronald Truluck wonders when you'll see him." She listened for ten seconds and said to Ronald, "You may enter."

Heavy drapes blocked all natural light in the inner office. Chief Smithers sat at attention behind his wide mahogany desk, with a state flag and an American flag behind him. A banker's lamp cast a spotlight on the desktop. Fleetwood sat in front of the desk with his legs crossed. After handshakes, Fleetwood rested his chin on his hand like he was already bored.

"Why are you here?" Ronald said to Fleetwood. "I have an appointment with Chief Smithers, not you."

"The chief requested I attend this summit."

"I wish you'd mentioned that in advance, Arthur," Ronald said. By addressing a bona fide adult authority figure by his first name, Ronald declared himself a participant in the rudeness competition. "I would have brought the newspaper lawyer with me."

Ronald knew the newspaper lawyer, Harry Waters, slightly. He had to calm down people who threatened to sue because Ronald put their name in the paper when they got arrested.

"If you want to call him, fine," Fleetwood said. "But since we're all here, why don't we go ahead and talk."

Addressing Chief Smithers, Ronald said, "I'm working on a story about Lamont Moody, the Millerton city council member."

"We all know who Lamont is," Fleetwood said. "Get to the point."

"I'm talking to the chief, not you." Ronald unfolded his notepad. "Lamont wrecked his car on July 31st on Archdale Street, early in the morning. I've asked for the accident report. Why haven't you made it public?"

"That incident is still under investigation, so the accident report is not available to the public yet," Chief Smithers said in a civics-lesson voice. "You see, it takes a long time to investigate a motor vehicle accident in the proper manner, and we want to make sure we have our ducks in a row before we conclude whether someone has broken the law. We take such accusations with great seriousness."

"There's a presumption of innocence," Fleetwood said.

"But there is an accident report." Ronald pulled out his copy and laid it on the chief's desk.

The chief repositioned the piece of paper with his index finger and folded his arms on his desk. His face clinched with an intense concentration that made Ronald's pulse quicken. The chief sat back and said, "Arthur?"

Fleetwood snatched up the accident report like it was one of ten thousand inconsequential pieces of paper that passed through his life every day. After a few seconds, he dropped it on the desk and said, "You're kidding, aren't you?"

"No," Ronald said, "I'm going to write a story about this wreck, and I'm doing you the courtesy of giving you a chance to respond."

"We can't stop you from doing that because we respect freedom of the press," Fleetwood said. "But a word of warning—you'll be making a fool of yourself."

"I don't think so."

"It's not an accident report until a law enforcement agency authenticates its truthfulness," Fleetwood said. "This is nothing more than a preliminary draft of an accident report. You'd be making a grave error to describe it as anything else. Where'd you get this?"

"I can't tell you the name of my source," Ronald said.

"Dwight Bennett," Chief Smithers said. He and Fleetwood laughed.

The office door opened. Ellen stepped inside and said, "What in the heck is so funny?"

"We asked Ronald where he got this accident report," Chief Smithers said, "and he told us ... he told us Dwight Bennett!"

Her eyes and mouth went round. "You're kidding me," she said.

"I didn't say it was Dwight!" Ronald yelled. They quieted down.

Chief Smithers pointed at the accident report and said, "But Dwight's name is right here at the bottom of the accident report."

"No, it's not," Ronald said.

He'd cut off the bottom of his copy of the report where Dwight wrote his signature. Even if everybody knew it was Dwight, Ronald looked slightly less dumb.

"Doesn't matter," Chief Smithers said. He flipped open the manila folder on his desk. "I've got Dwight's personnel records right here in front of me. I can't let you look at them, but I can tell you it's not a good idea to use him as a source in any kind of story."

"I'd like you to give me a copy of those records," Ronald said. He should have requested Dwight's personnel records already.

"Personnel files are confidential. All that was off the record. I told you because I don't want you stepping into a pile of crap."

The chief was trying to retroactively go off the record. Amateur move. Conversations were only off the record if the source and the reporter agreed on those terms before the conversation started. At least, that's what Ronald learned in journalism school. If Ronald reported what the chief said, he'd be in the clear ethically, but if he reported Dwight's previous infractions, he'd be undercutting his source's credibility. Ronald had just outsmarted himself.

"I didn't say Dwight was the source, but if he was such a problem, why didn't you fire him earlier?" Ronald said.

"Dwight's a war hero. That counts for something in my book."

They were also unaware Dwight might have fooled everybody with Vietnam.

"Did you fire him because he was sleeping with the mayor's daughter?" Ronald asked.

Chief Smithers and Fleetwood looked at each other. Ellen Swicegood sighed and left the office.

"We're not saying why Dwight left the department," Fleetwood said. "We respect men who served in the military and would never do anything to make life difficult for a veteran."

"Did you bury the accident report because Lamont's on the council?"

Chief Smithers' face hardened into a stone mask. His cop stare was the best Ronald had encountered. On the other side of the country, criminals twitched.

"That," Chief Smithers said, "is an extremely serious accusation. It implies I have tried to help a lawbreaker evade the consequences of their actions. It implies I am not a good police officer. It implies I am dishonest. Look at me, Ronald." The chief's white shirt accentuated the pinkening of his Irish scowl. "Is that what you think about me? That I am dishonest?"

"I didn't say you did that, I *asked* if you did," Ronald said. "Because I want to know what happened. Why didn't you arrest Lamont?"

"Because the chief wasn't out investigating wrecks after midnight," Fleetwood said.

"I'm talking about the plural you," Ronald said. "I'm talking about the department."

"We got us an English major here," Fleetwood said. "He knows his way around the English language."

"So why didn't the police take in Lamont for drunk driving?" Ronald said.

Chief Smithers tapped his fingers on his desktop like he was playing soft notes on a piano.

"I've said everything I'm going to say. Goodbye, Ronald."

Ronald left. As he walked down the corridor, Joe Stoneman came out of the squad room and walked toward him. Ronald nodded hello. As they neared each other, Stoneman took a big step out of his lane and delivered an upright body block that sent Ronald stumbling. He banged his head against the wall and dropped his notebook. Stoneman didn't stop. "Watch where I'm going," he called over his shoulder.

CHAPTER TWENTY

Ronald rushed back to the newsroom and found a young Black man sitting at the desk of Lewis Daisy, the photographer, reading *The Eagle* like he belonged there.

"This is Marcus James," Martha said. "He's filling in as photographer while Lewis takes time off for cancer treatment."

"Lewis has cancer?"

"We talked about it at the staff meeting this morning. The meeting you missed."

"It's great to be here," Marcus said, executing a facsimile of a smile. As the first Black person to work in *The Eagle* newsroom, he was the Jackie Robinson of Millerton journalism. Marcus dressed in the kind of clothes Ronald hadn't worn since the eleventh grade: Polyester slacks, a short-sleeved dress shirt, black tie, and dress shoes.

"Welcome to *The Eagle*," Ronald said, raising his hand for a thumbs-interlocking soul shake to establish their solidarity as Black man and white long hair. But Marcus angled his hand downward and they performed a traditional shake. It was a safe move for a first day on the job, but Ronald didn't like the implication he was a standard-issue Caucasian.

Ronald told Mr. Carlton and Martha about his interviews with Lamont and the chief. They were alarmed he talked to Chief Smithers without clearing it with them, but they got over it after he told them Lamont offered to write a check for damages.

"That's not quite a real confession, but it's close," Martha said.

"We might be able to go with the accident report after all," Mr. Carlton said. "I think it's real. But I'm serious about needing some sort of eyewitness quotes, either an officer or a citizen. We've got to show proper respect for elected officials. They're not just regular Joes."

Mr. Carlton's respect for the democratic process was dragging Ronald down. The Jorgensens wouldn't talk, and Dwight was still off the record. That put the story at a standstill, but he didn't feel discouraged. He had an irrational confidence something would happen to keep Lamontgate alive.

Ronald telephoned the National Archives in St. Louis, got the address, and typed up the request for Dwight's military records. He put a stamp on the envelope and dropped it into the outgoing mail basket, which Linda would take to the post office at noon. Ronald hoped she didn't sniff out that the letter concerned Dwight, her secret flame.

Marcus accompanied Ronald on his next assignment, a feature about Hawk Hawkins, the sheriff. As they walked to the sheriff's department, Marcus explained he was taking a semester off from North Carolina Central, the Black college in Durham, where he'd been the sports editor and chief photographer for the student paper. This was his first paying news job. He was twenty years old, meaning Ronald was no longer the youngest in the office.

The sheriff's department was a block from the courthouse with offices attached to the seventy-five-bed jail. Hawk's weathered face cracked into a smile when Ronald and Marcus entered his office. He wore his trademark outfit—cowboy boots and a western shirt with a bolo tie cinched at the neck with a special clasp. Today it was an arrowhead. The feature was about Hawk's collection of tie clasps, which were mounted on small hooks on a board attached to a wall. He had clasps of American flags, North Carolina flags, Confederate flags, hawks and other birds of prey, deer and other forest animals, police badges, polished stones, guns, crossed swords, trucks, and police cars. Mr. Carlton said people gave Hawk the clasps as a way of sucking up. When Ronald asked how Hawk got away with not wearing a standard uniform, Mr. Carlton said, "Because he's the sheriff."

Hawk gave Ronald a high-action handshake, then threw his arms around Marcus.

"How's your mother doing?" Hawk said. "I'm glad to see she's keeping the school board in line."

"She's fine and sends her love. How's your family, Sheriff?"

Ronald understood how Marcus got the job. He was the son of Millie James, the first Black member of the county school board and therefore the highest Black official in the county, not to mention the most-quoted Black person in *The Eagle*.

The interview was a success. Hawk reeled off good quotes. Marcus shot pictures of Hawk holding tie clasps while wearing his cowboy hat. During the interview, a man in a khaki deputy's uniform entered the office without knocking and sat against the wall, watching with icy blue eyes. Sammy Nichols was chief deputy, the number two in the sheriff's department. He directed the nitty-gritty cop work while Hawk politicked. Nichols made Ronald nervous.

"How are my good friends at the police department doing?" Hawk said when the interview had ended. "I hear Chief Smithers wants to build a new police station."

Gossip time. Ronald needed to be careful not to disturb the surface story that the sheriff's department and the Millerton police held each other in the deepest respect. The police were rankled because the sheriff's department had countywide jurisdiction. Every few months deputies made an arrest in the city when a bad guy crossed from the county into the city limits. The sheriff's department seethed because Chief Smithers supposedly called Hawk a showboat.

Ronald explained how Lamont had changed his position on the feasibility study for the police station.

"That sounds like something Lamont would do," Hawk said. "The county commission bought a backhoe from him a few years ago, and he kept trying to change the price, even after the contract was signed. Another thing I heard is that you've been asking some questions about a wreck Lamont had."

Ronald didn't want to talk about his investigation until he was ready to publish.

"Some," he said.

"The police department has hired a couple of my deputies in the last couple of years," Hawk said. "Do you know Joe Stoneman?"

"I've seen him around the police station."

Hawk and Sammy kept staring. Ronald felt a compulsion to say more.

"He's pulled me over two times, but he didn't give me a ticket."

Hawk nodded. "Between you and me, we had to let Joe go because he violated some protocols during traffic stops. I asked the chief not to hire Joe, but he went ahead and did it anyway. I wish he hadn't."

Ronald was unnerved. Cops hated to admit that a cop had done something wrong, even a cop from another department. The occupational protectiveness was too strong. That Hawk did so proved the schism between the departments was deeper than Ronald had imagined.

"Joe got a little physical with me," Ronald said. "And he let me know I should back off reporting Lamont."

"You need to be careful out there," Hawk said with a smile, as if he was saying Ronald should look both ways before crossing the street. He continued, "Hey, all that stuff about the police department and Joe and Lamont, we were just talking. You know what I mean."

Like the chief, Hawk was retroactively trying to put the conversation off the record. Ronald would let it go. He knew he needed to stay on Hawk's good side.

CHAPTER TWENTY-ONE

Ellen Swicegood called not long after Ronald got back to the newsroom.

"Ronald, I guess you've already heard about the wreck last night. I wanted to make sure you got the information before the other reporters. If you come up to the chief's office, I can let you see the accident report."

Ronald had heard about the wreck, a one-car fatal, from the ambulance service. He was going to ask about it when he visited Betty Stokes at the police station. Ronald knew why Ellen was being nice. The power dynamic had shifted. Ronald had the accident report on Lamont, putting him beyond the chief's control. When he walked into the chief's office, Ellen handed him an accident report and asked if she could get him a cup of coffee.

The typed report said the wreck happened at 11:14 the previous night when a red Ford Mustang traveled down Railroad Street at a high rate of speed while being pursued by police. The car went out of control and plowed into a utility pole, causing it to catch fire and kill the driver, identified as Joe Butler, 55, of Magnolia Lane. Earlier in the night, Butler stole the car from the driveway of the owner, Travis Sprinkle, 19, of Hunter Street.

Ronald recorded the information in his notebook. He held up the report. "Could I get a copy of this?"

Chief Smithers emerged from his office and said, "This is a public document, but we wanted to give *The Eagle* a head start on the story, before the other newspapers and TV stations. We know how competitive things can get in the media, so we're not going to put this accident report on the clipboard until tomorrow. Millerton people need to look out for each other. Don't you agree?"

They shook. No bone crusher.

"You know, Ronald, our relationship has gotten off on the wrong foot," the chief said. "We don't need to be butting heads. We both have the same goal: to make Millerton a great place to live. I respect the press, and I think you respect the police. Why don't we start all over with mutual respect?"

"I still need the Archdale Street accident report."

"But that wreck is inconsequential. Nobody was hurt. In this one, a man was killed. He's not on the city council, but he's still a man. He has a family. Isn't this wreck more important?"

Ronald stood firm, like a statue of Joseph Pulitzer. Chief Smithers sighed.

"Well, let me check with Arthur Fleetwood. Maybe we can get something for you soon."

Ronald and Marcus went out to find pictures for the wreck story, which was designated the lead for the next day's front page. Ronald schooled the rookie as he drove.

"You'll end up shooting a lot of grip and grins and check presentations," he said. "Like Eagle Scouts and kids having perfect attendance in school. An occasional wreck."

"Exciting stuff. I specialize in portraits, not just important people but regular folks. That's what I want to shoot."

Ronald didn't tell him *The Eagle* didn't run many portraits. They found half a dozen people gathered at the accident site admiring the scarred and charred utility pole. Ronald got quotes and wrote the story. It had been a good day, with the chief and Ellen Swicegood acknowledging his power and influence.

After work, he and Monica drove to Winston-Salem to see *The Great Gatsby*. It hadn't come to the Millerton theater yet. They went back to her house since her parents were still at the beach. She started talking about the novel the movie was based on, which she'd read fifteen times and written four college papers on. It sounded like she was reciting from her papers. Since he'd only read the book twice, she wouldn't listen to anything he had to say. That was irritating, but he still spent the night.

CHAPTER TWENTY-TWO

Ronald arrived at work the next day to find Mr. Carlton and Martha talking to a man in a work shirt. He had a red face and glared like Ronald had just run over his best dog, backed up, and run over it again.

"This is Joe Butler," Mr. Carlton said.

"You're not dead?" Ronald said. "The police say you're dead. The accident report says you're dead. My story says you're dead." The front page of *The Eagle* was spread across Mr. Carlton's desk. "Car Thief Perishes in Fiery Crash," shrieked the headline.

"Travis Sprinkle is dead, but people think I'm dead because of your stupid story," Butler said. "The ladies from church are bringing food by the house. I've had crying women in my living room all morning. My wife is humiliated. How could you mix up the names like that?"

"I didn't mix them up. The police did. They're the ones who said you were driving the car. I copied down everything on the accident report."

"I've already talked to the police, and they say the opposite. They say you're the one who messed up. They say you have a reputation for messing up. On top of all that, people think I've been stealing cars. The guys at the shop got my picture and put this on the bulletin board."

Butler slapped a piece of paper on the desk. It was a handmade poster that showed his picture under the words "Wanted for Car Theft."

"Why'd they make the poster if they thought you were dead?" Ronald said.

"Because they're making fun of me. One of them called my house to ask my wife what happened, and I answered the phone. That's how they found out."

Ronald picked up the fake poster and read the small print. It said Butler weighed five hundred pounds, had tattoos of one hundred twenty naked women on his chest, and should be considered armed but not dangerous because "he can't shoot worth shit."

"You've stolen my good name," Butler said. "I'll never live this down. Hippie college boys like you don't know a thief from an honest, hardworking citizen."

Mr. Carlton employed his soothing voice and agreed a correction was warranted. Butler shook hands with the editor but ignored Ronald's outstretched palm. "And it's a 1970 Mustang, not a '71," he said. "Fix that while you're at it."

As soon as Butler slammed the door, Mr. Carlton and Martha swiveled toward Ronald, creating a wall of judgment.

"I didn't mix up the names," Ronald said. "This is subterfuge. Ellen Swicegood and Chief Smithers are trying to ruin me to stop my story about Lamont."

"Run to the police station," Martha commanded. "Get a copy of the accident report and bring it back."

Ronald sprinted across the parking lot. Betty, dressed in her normal uniform, handed him the clipboard with the fatal accident report on top. It said the opposite of what Ronald's story said. It said Joe Butler owned the car and Travis Sprinkle stole it. It said Travis Sprinkle was killed. It said Ronald had been screwed.

"They changed the report," he whispered to Betty. She patted him on the arm.

"I told you Ellen was evil," Betty whispered back. "And look who wrote the report." The signature on the bottom said Joe Stoneman. "This is a conspiracy against you, Scoop. You need to fight back."

"I could get fired for this. Will you tell my bosses they changed the accident report behind my back?" he said.

She shook her head no, then made Ronald a copy of the official accident report that said Joe Butler wasn't dead. When he walked out of the police station, a van with the words "Channel 5 Action News" painted on the side pulled into the parking lot. The passenger door opened. A woman planted her high heels on the asphalt and slammed the van door with a wrist flick. With rippling blonde hair and powder-blue blazer, Dawn Mourning lit up Millerton like a small sun. She approached the police department doors followed by a schlub carrying a heavy TV camera and stopped in front of Ronald. He still held the accident report in his hand. Up close, her lipstick was an unnatural shade of red.

"I guess you're covering the wreck too," she said in a flat, midwestern accent. "Sounds bad. I've got an interview in ten minutes with Smithers. Who are you with?"

"*The Eagle.* I'm Ronald Truluck. I've already written a story about the wreck."

"Ouch," she said. "Smithers told me on the phone. That's a tough break."

"I didn't get it wrong. They gave me a bogus report to make me look bad."

"Why would they do that?" She cocked her head a few degrees to convey curiosity.

He wasn't about to hand her Lamontgate. "Long story. Maybe I'll have time to tell you one day."

Ronald ascended the steps to the second-floor newsroom. A bald man wearing a baggy business suit paced back and forth in front of Mr. Carlton's desk with one hand in his pocket. That was Harry Waters, the newspaper lawyer.

"Your reporter is calling the police chief and a city councilman liars but he can't decide if Joe Butler is dead or alive," Waters said.

Ronald didn't call anybody a liar, just implied it. He started to clear up that point, but Martha tightened her lips as a signal to shut up. Ronald retreated to his desk.

"Do you know Doug Saget in Raleigh, the state rep?" Waters asked. "He called me an hour ago. He's a libel lawyer and represents Lamont. Said Lamont's thinking about filing suit against *The Eagle*."

Mr. Carlton rocked back and forth in his office chair with his hands clasped. Ronald had read a book titled *Body Language* while killing time in the library. Mr. Carlton had assumed a defensive posture. He was not winning the conversation.

"What kind of stuff do you have on Lamont?" Waters said. He laid both palms on the edge of Mr. Carlton's desk. Mr. Carlton told him about the accident report and the interviews.

"You don't have any official police documents? Is that what you're saying?"

"We don't have official documents because the police have not issued the accident report," Mr. Carlton said, unlocking his fingers and waving his hands. He was now the defender of the document he once questioned. "We have the accident report. It just doesn't have the police department's seal of approval, but it was given to us by the police officer who prepared the report."

"Former police officer," Waters said, and started pacing again. "Dwight Bennett. That's your source? Wow."

"We're not publicly identifying the source," Ronald said. They looked at him like he'd materialized out of the carpet.

"I know Dwight's done some questionable things, but let's remember he went through a lot in Vietnam," Mr. Carlton said. "I heard he was a prisoner of war for six months. Isn't that right, Ronald?"

The rumors were wilder than Ronald imagined. How long would it take to get Dwight's military records?

"I've spent hours interviewing Dwight, and he's an open book about almost everything, but he doesn't talk much about his combat, I mean, his military experiences," Ronald said.

"Maybe he's shell-shocked," Waters said. He wasn't bald. He had an almost invisible combover. Ronald's phone rang. It was Dwight.

"What the hell!" he screamed. "Two of my buddies in the police department called to say Chief Smithers knows I've been talking to you. Did you tell him? Because if you did I'm going to sue your ass off. I'm going to ..."

"I didn't tell him."

"Everybody says you did. They're saying ..."

Ronald hung up. The phone rang ten seconds later. He knew it was Dwight, apoplectic with anger. Ronald unplugged the phone.

"Listen, I.J., I'm not telling you what to do," Waters said. "You're the editor, and I'm the lawyer. If you had some more stuff about Lamont, some witnesses, and sources other than Dwight, I'd feel a lot better about your Lamont story. Right now, it seems kind of thin."

"You're right about one thing. I am the editor and you are the lawyer."

"And as your lawyer, I'm duty bound to say if you run this story, you'll get sued. I don't feel real confident about *The Eagle*'s chances. If a lawyer gets Dwight Bennett on the witness stand, it could be a disaster. And Ronald, well, I think cross-examination might be tough on him. And this new mistake he made"—he spoke like Ronald wasn't in the room—"is embarrassing as hell."

Mr. Carlton stood up and walked around to the front of his desk.

"We don't know what happened with this name mix-up. It may not be our fault. And nobody's filed a lawsuit yet." They shook hands. "Let me think about what you said."

After the lawyer left, Mr. Carlton sat fidgeting with his eyepatch. Then he and Martha stood at the window looking at city hall across the parking lot. Ronald stared at a blank piece of paper in the typewriter. He was about to be fired from a pipsqueak paper. If that happened, he wouldn't clean out his desk or return to his apartment. He'd drive away and wander the world working blue-collar jobs the rest of his life. He'd never come back to North Carolina.

Martha walked over and lowered herself into the chair next to Ronald's desk.

"Is TV covering the wreck?" she asked.

"Yes, Dawn Mourning of Channel 5. She's interviewing the chief right now."

"Great. You know how I.J. hates that. But the main thing is we believe the chief and Ellen faked the accident report. It was a terrible and dishonest thing for them to do," she said.

"Thank you. I'm not lying. I wish I could prove it to you. They're doing it to derail my investigation of Lamont. When I showed the chief and Arthur Fleetwood the accident report I got from Dwight, they were shocked. They freaked out. They're desperate to stop this story."

"I have my own sources at city hall. They let me know there was some sort of hanky-panky."

"Who's your source?"

"Dot Smith in the city manager's office. We're good friends."

Martha wouldn't take Ronald's word for it. That hurt. She needed confirmation from Dot.

"What are we going to do about it? Are you and Mr. Carlton going over to the chief's office to demand an explanation and an apology?" he said.

"If we had a copy of the fake report, we would. But we don't. It's your word against theirs. We couldn't win that argument."

"We can't quit, Martha. We don't have to win, but we need to put up a fight. We can't lie down for them."

"We can't afford to take that attitude," she said. "We've got to keep the paper alive. As for the Lamont story, we're not intimidated by Chief Smithers or what Harry Waters says, but we do need more reporting. We need eyewitnesses to the wreck. Somebody somewhere will talk. We want to be rock solid, because it's a serious accusation to say the police covered up a wreck just because Lamont is on the city council. You need to revisit your sources and see if you can shake something loose. We're not quitting this story, even if it takes us ten years to get it."

Martha couldn't look him in the face. She was a journalist to the bone and therefore lousy at public relations. She and Mr. Carlton would never admit it, but they were giving up. They were talking tough while retreating.

CHAPTER TWENTY-THREE

"I wish I'd been fired," Ronald told Monica. "That would have been conclusive. Now I've got to cover the police every day knowing they're laughing at me. Should I resign?"

Monica slumped into the sofa cushions. "Sometimes you have to live with indecision," she said. She didn't offer any advice on what to do next. She seemed as confused and defeated as he was.

Sex seemed like the logical next step, but Monica suggested they go to another movie and went to shower. None of the movies at the two-screen Millerton theater were any good so Ronald spread *The Winston-Salem Guardian* on the kitchen counter to check the movie ads. He was imagining a trip to see her at college in Florida—and enjoying waterbed sex in an apartment decorated with Joni Mitchell posters—when the doorbell rang. He went to the foyer. Through the narrow windows beside the door he saw a short, balding man holding a briefcase. Perhaps the last of the door-to-door salesmen. It might be fun to hasten his extinction.

"May I speak with Monica Timbes?" said the little man. He was about forty and wore pressed polyester slacks and a white dress shirt tucked in at the waist. The goatee was the only thing that disqualified him from the ranks of the average man. "I'm Dr. Barry Fussell."

"You're making a house call?"

"I'm not that kind of doctor. I have a doctorate in literature." He peeked into the house.

"Where do you teach?" Ronald leaned against the doorframe.

"The University of Florida."

"You must be one of Monica's professors."

"I do work at the university. And you are ..."

"Ronald Truluck. Monica's friend."

He didn't have a good word to describe their relationship. He didn't want to say they were "dating" because dating was a sexist anachronism. "Friend" was an understatement. He didn't want to say "boyfriend" until they came to an understanding.

"May I come inside, Ronald?" For a small guy, Barry had a penetrating voice. He stepped into the foyer and looked around. "The place hasn't changed much. I've been here twice, for Thanksgiving and Christmas, but I have a photographic memory. How are Hugh and Diane?"

"They're fine. Are you here to talk to Monica about her dissertation?"

"I'm here to talk about her future. Shall we go into the living room?"

Ronald had no objections to the living room, but he needed to break Barry's reign of control. "In here," Ronald said and led Barry to the kitchen. After filling a water glass, Ronald looked up to find the mystery man drilling into him with intense brown eyes. Barry was two inches and ten pounds smaller than Ronald and had a smooth, shining head devoid of knicks and scars, like he'd never bumped into a brick wall. If it came to it, Ronald could take him.

"So, how long have you been Monica's *friend*?" Barry said.

Before he could answer, Monica bustled into the kitchen wearing a terry cloth bathrobe and radiating heat from the shower.

"Barry, what are you doing here? This is crazy. I wish you hadn't come."

He lifted his arms, like she'd step in for a hug, but she didn't go for it.

"I drove all the way from Gainesville—and a beastly drive it is—because you haven't answered my phone calls or letters. We have business to take care of, dearest Monica, and I'd like to do so posthaste." He cut his eyes at Ronald. "Could we go somewhere for a private moment? Perhaps Hugh's office?"

"Who is this guy?" Ronald said. "He acts like he owns the place."

Monica and Barry looked at each other.

"I'm her husband," Barry said. "Soon to be her ex-husband, if she'll put her Joanna Hancock on these divorce papers in my briefcase."

Married? Monica didn't wear a wedding ring and never mentioned her marital status, such as saying, "Your sex drive exceeds that of my estranged husband." Monica gazed out the kitchen window, the down on her face glistening in the sunlight. She had the nerve to look sexy at a moment like this.

"You didn't tell me you were married," he said.

"I said I wasn't dating anybody, and that's the truth," she said. "And besides, it's none of your business if I'm married or not."

They'd exchanged enough bodily fluids to make it his business. He'd been conned. While marriage was a meaningless institution, having sex with a married woman was not something he planned to do. It could get you killed.

"Monica, you withheld important information from me. That's the same thing as lying," Ronald said. In a further attempt to make himself the victim, he added, "You turned me into an adulterer."

"Not necessarily," Barry said. "I'm not sure what North Carolina law stipulates, but under most religious laws, the married person is the adulterer whereas you, Ronald, are a fornicator. Ethically, I think you're in the clear."

"Cool it, Barry," Monica said. "This is one of the reasons we're getting divorced. You're so anal about language."

"Being precise with language is my job, Monica, and I'm the one who's divorcing you." Barry unsnapped the briefcase, pulled out a sheath of papers, and dropped them on the kitchen counter. "Sign these. Let's get this over with."

She didn't touch the papers. "I'll read them and ask my father to read them, and if they're all right, I'll sign and mail them back. I don't like to be rushed. You know me."

"I don't know you at all," Barry said, stepping closer. His voice harshened. "I do know you've had three months to read the papers. I do know you ran away from Gainesville to avoid the inevitable."

"I didn't run away and don't tell me what to do. Get out!"

"Not without your signature." Barry grabbed the papers and pushed them toward her.

Ronald's ingrained ethical code would not allow him to stand by while a woman was physically threatened by a man smaller than he was. He stepped between them and puffed out his chest, a macho reflex that could only intimidate a shrimp like Barry.

"You better leave," Ronald said, "or things could get rough."

"Please, Ronald. We're not going to fight over this. We're both intelligent men."

Ronald balled his fists. "I'm not an intelligent man."

"Okay, okay, I'll leave." Barry held up both hands and stepped back. Ronald continued to radiate silent hostility toward the invader who threatened his home and his woman—except he didn't live in the house and had no idea where he stood with Monica. "Cheerio," Barry said and exited the kitchen.

Monica and Ronald glared at each other until the front door shut and the motor on Barry's car started. Maybe they'd follow up the argument with volcanic makeup sex on the kitchen floor. The breakfast table was also an option. Monica tightened her bathrobe belt and squared her shoulders.

"So now you're throwing people out of my house. You've got a lot of nerve. Who in the hell do you think you are?"

"You're the nervy one, trying to put me on the defensive when you're in the wrong. And I'll tell you who I am: the guy who deserves some answers."

She filled a glass with water at the sink and took a sip, then walked to Ronald and laid her palm on his chest. "You do deserve some answers."

They sat down in the breakfast nook for their first real relationship talk. He was at a disadvantage because he hadn't prepared his arguments. Women never had to prepare. They were born talking about relationships.

He was hoping for a cop brief explanation but got an epic novel instead. As he figured, it was a grad student-professor love affair. Barry, who was brilliant, taught twentieth century American literature at the University of Florida. She took one of his classes and asked the right questions. She helped him organize papers and he advised her on her dissertation. Barry and Monica went to a wine bar. They went to a Greek restaurant. They went to the beach. They fell in love. They moved into a house with a tin roof and a flower garden.

"We were happy," she said and leaned back in her chair as if concluding a segment of the conversation. But she wasn't telling everything—he could feel it. Painful facts were deleted.

"What you've given me," Ronald said, "is a modified limited hangout."

"A what?"

"That's a famous phrase from Watergate, spoken by John Ehrlichman, one of Nixon's aides. Somebody tells part of the truth to avoid confessing the whole truth."

He figured she'd know what he meant. She talked about Watergate all the time and how it symbolized everything wrong with America.

She said, "Are you calling me a liar, like Nixon?"

"I'm asking, was Barry married?" Ronald said, a cop interrogating a suspect. Not his intended tone, but that's how it came out.

Monica pulled her robe closer. Barry's wife, Clarice, was not a terrible person, but she was cold and distant—and a banker, not an academic, not a person attuned to literature like they were—so the marriage was dead from the beginning. No kids. The implication: minimal damage.

"Why did you even marry Barry? Why not live together?"

They scrutinized each other across the table. Monica's breath smelled good. Her personal ethics were suspect, but her personal hygiene was exemplary.

"We figured why not? It would simplify our finances and just make life easier," she said.

Practical and in line with Ronald's belief that marriage was just a piece of paper. Maybe he was overreacting. Maybe this is how real life happened— messy and not always making sense. But the reporter in him wanted things to make sense even as she rested her warm foot on top of his under the table.

"And then you split up. Why?"

Monica clasped her hands and held them to her chin, a prayer-like pose, as if telling was going to hurt. Barry changed. He turned mean and spiteful as soon as they said, "I do." Putting her down in front of their friends. Stopped helping with her dissertation. Holding up the things she loved for hypercritical analysis, like she was an academic rival. He ripped into the Beatles, for God's sake. Who could hate the Beatles? The seventeen-year age difference helped doom their marriage.

That would never happen with Ronald. Marrying someone seventeen years older would be a generational act of treason.

"The marriage was a big mistake," she said, giving him the full, come-inside-my-brain eyeball treatment. "We were only married a year and a half. I had to get out for my sanity. You know what it's like to be stuck in a terrible relationship."

He didn't know. He'd never *been* in any kind of relationship, except for those few weeks with Beth Medford in college. But Monica had wrecked Barry's first marriage. She was about to end her own marriage. She might have dumped a dozen guys. She had an advanced degree in relationships and Ronald, a GED.

"I've changed my mind about the movie," Monica said. She put her water glass in the sink. The goodbye kiss was quick and dry.

CHAPTER
TWENTY-FOUR

For two days, Ronald went about his business while trying to decide whether to quit his job and break up with Monica. He covered the police beat. Made chitchat with Betty Stokes. Had snippy conversations with Linda Lasseter. Had every syllable he wrote scrutinized by Martha. At night, he got stoned and listened to records at Snap's house. He spilled his guts to Shelly over lunch at the Millerton Diner.

"I'm not saying marriage is important," he said. "It's an antiquated institution designed to subjugate women and restrict sexual freedom. It was the way Monica withheld information that bothers me so much. I don't know if I can date her anymore."

"You're right, she should have told you," Shelly said. "While the sexual revolution has changed male-female relations on a permanent basis, there are still unwritten rules of dating, and she broke one of them. If you have an emotional, sexual, or legal entanglement with somebody else, you're obligated to tell the person you're dating."

He felt better. Shelly, also a relationships expert, confirmed Monica had done him wrong.

"If you'd known Monica was married but separated, would you have dated her?" Shelly said.

"Yes, once I determined her husband wasn't a homicidal maniac. But she didn't tell me. Personal honesty is very important to me. I want an apology."

The conversation paused while the waitress limped up to their booth with chicken sandwiches, which turned out to be fried chicken wings on dry hamburger buns. Ronald had anticipated something more, like a cutlet between two pieces of Italian bread, but he went ahead and ate it. Another Millerton oddity.

"Are you overreacting?" Shelly said. "So far, you two have had sex a few times. That doesn't make her your true-blue girlfriend. How can you break up with somebody when you're not in a relationship with them? And listen to yourself—you just said marriage is a meaningless institution, so if she didn't tell you she was married, what does it matter? What she did is forgivable, in my opinion, considering how much you like her."

"I can't trust her," Ronald said.

"You're not in the trust stage. You're in the lust stage. Talk to her, but don't demand an apology. You're happier since you started going out with Monica. As far as quitting your job, I hope you don't, but if you do quit, you'll find another one at another small paper. You should worry about Monica more than your job."

Shelly made sense, but a few hours later he reconsidered. Was it a good idea to take relationship advice from somebody who got the name wrong in the pet-of-the-week photo caption? She said it was Cuddles when it should have been Bubbles. The animal control director complained and asked for a correction, but Mr. Carlton stood firm. *The Eagle* had never run a correction on a cat's name and never would while he was in charge.

Ronald came up with a triple option strategy for Monica. He'd meet her at a neutral location so she couldn't make a scene, then start with small talk. Movies and books were good subjects. He'd check *The New York Times* bestseller list so he could hold up his end of the conversation. He'd bring up the subject of Barry, the husband she forgot to mention. If she apologized, he'd forgive her. If she told him to mind his own business, he'd walk into the sunset. If she was somewhere in between, he'd go with his gut. He called

Monica the next morning and asked her to meet at the picnic tables at Lake Miller that afternoon.

"We're giving my grandmother a birthday party tonight and I need to pick up some flowers. How about I swing by *The Eagle* office, and we can talk while I drive."

That deviated from his plan and ceded an important control point to Monica, but they had always talked best while riding around town. She was late. As he stood outside the paper, his sense of being deceived deepened. Maybe she wasn't coming just to make him feel ridiculous. Then her Corolla turned the corner and he got into the passenger seat. She wore sunglasses and had tied her hair into a ponytail.

"What a weird scene with Barry," she said before Ronald could even ask if she'd read *Watership Down*, a British novel about a society of highly conversant rabbits. That killed his chance of doing Bugs Bunny with an English accent. "I couldn't believe he just showed up. Sorry you had to go through that."

There it was—an offhand, half-hearted apology, like she'd set the thermostat too high. He wasn't satisfied.

"Why didn't you tell me you were married?" he said.

For the next mile she looked back and forth between him and the road but didn't say anything. She pulled into a parking spot in front of Nancy's Flowers, cut the engine, and took off her sunglasses.

"You're right, it was wrong of me. I've been trying to forget about Barry. I couldn't bring myself to talk about him with anybody, even the people I care about." Her chin crumpled. "I thought if I did tell you that you wouldn't want anything to do with me, and I guess I was right because you're about to dump me. I was a chicken. I was going to tell you soon."

She nestled her fingers inside his palm. It was a nice move, considering she'd inched closer to an actual apology, but it didn't go far enough for Ronald. He was about to drop the bomb and incinerate her psyche like Nagasaki when she said, "I felt so bad about it I did something I told you I wouldn't. I called Bill Jorgensen."

Jorgensen, the silent witness who could unlock the Lamont Moody story. Ronald asked, hating himself, "What did he say?"

"He was a terrible teacher, but I guess I'm one of his success stories since he put the idea of majoring in English in my head. I said, 'Let's have lunch,' and we got together at The Baker's Dozen. We talked about books and writing. I can do that all day long. I didn't tell him I know you. I mentioned Lamont because I just saw his picture in the paper doing something. Bill said Lamont was a good guy and helped him get a job with the city recreation department."

"He works for the city? I didn't know that. What else did he say?"

"I asked how he happened to know Lamont and he said everybody knows Lamont. Which is true. Later in the day, I went to the library to check out some books and I found Bill sitting in the reading room, writing in a notebook. We went outside and sat on the bench talking for an hour and a half. We'd already had a two-hour lunch. I said, 'You're not having to punch the clock, are you?' and he laughed."

"Jorgensen wants to talk, but his wife won't let him for some reason. Could Lamont have bought their silence with a crummy job? Did you get that idea?"

"Bill has always had trouble holding jobs. He tried to tutor, and nobody hired him. His head is in the clouds all the time. He says he's going to publish a second book of poetry." She hooted. "I can't imagine what that will be like."

A new avenue of investigation. If Jorgensen got a do-nothing job in exchange for staying quiet about the wreck, the corruption in Millerton went deeper than Ronald imagined. Just like Watergate, it was the cover-up, not the crime, that would bring down the criminals.

"I know I said earlier that I couldn't stand to talk to Bill, but I felt like I owed you one after what I did. I want to help."

He couldn't break up with her now. This tip was better than a weeping apology. Lamontgate was back on track. His whole life was getting back on track.

"Get the flowers," Ronald said. "Then we'll talk about what movie to see this weekend."

CHAPTER
TWENTY-FIVE

Nobody answered when Ronald knocked on the front door at the scene of the crime. Flowers had been planted around the river rocks circling the new birdbath. Grass had grown over the tire tracks. He found Sarah Jorgensen hoeing the vegetable garden in the backyard.

"You're back." She stood with both her hands on top of the hoe handle.

He'd seen her in this clothing combination before: jeans rolled up at the ankles and a men's T-shirt falling below her hips. The same aggrieved expression.

"I wanted to ask you again about the night Lamont wrecked in your front yard. I've got the accident report." She twitched, almost a flinch. "I've talked to the cop who was on the scene. I know Lamont insulted you. Are you going to let him get away with that?"

She looked away. "No comment. That's all I'm saying."

The concrete bowl of the old birdbath sat on two cinder blocks in the middle of the backyard, about fifteen feet away. He looked at it, which caused her to look at it too.

"Did Lamont pay for the new one out front? That sounds like taking a bribe to me. Maybe I should speak with the man of the house."

"Bill's at work."

"Which park?"

"I didn't say where he worked."

"I'll ask at the recreation department."

She resumed chopping the dirt. "Check his office at Candler Park."

Candler Park had two tennis courts with sagging nets, a basketball court with no nets on the rims, and a small playground. The one building was an equipment shed. According to the police, the Black crime lords of Millerton congregated there on Saturday night to sell truckloads of marijuana, though they only got arrested for possessing joints. When Ronald arrived, two women watched toddlers in a sandbox. He crossed to the low-slung shed with a door made of corrugated metal, which swung open when he tapped on it. The inside smelled of soil, cut grass, and gasoline—a reminder of Ronald's landscaping days between college semesters. He called Jorgensen's name. Nobody answered. He felt around on the wall and found the light switch.

The room had a red dirt floor with half a dozen push mowers lined up in loose formation. Hand tools hung from numbered hooks on the wall. A wooden desk was in the corner, the kind an elementary school teacher would use, with a folding metal chair. He sat down and switched on a lamp. Papers were stacked in wire baskets. The brass nameplate said William R. Jorgensen.

Under a clipboard, Ronald found a legal pad filled with doodles of battleships and fighter jets and bursts of poetry about languid lips and simmering sunsets and tart tongues. It was sentimental stuff, something Ronald's mother would have written if she'd been the poetry type. He opened desk drawers. Three more legal pads filled with doodles and poetry, with each page dated in the top right corner. Worn paperbacks of poetry by Robert Frost and Carl Sandberg—the poetry Ronald tried to make himself like in college. He found a 1952 yearbook from Elon College with Jorgensen's mug shot. His plastered-down hair was thinning at the temples, foreshadowing an adulthood of baldness. His pinched, thin lips begged to never be kissed.

Underneath the yearbook, Ronald found a checkbook with a blue leather cover. He didn't open it. Rifling the drawers was allowable because the desk was public property, but not the checkbook. It contained private secrets that would help Ronald break the story, such as Jorgensen's pay, but Ronald would be crossing an ethical line if he looked at a single entry. He wouldn't sacrifice his integrity for a mere story. Then the door opened, and Bill Jorgensen walked in.

"What the hell!" Jorgensen shouted. "Put down my checkbook!"

Ronald dropped the checkbook and slammed the drawer shut. He stood. Jorgensen took two steps forward, then two steps sideways, looking Ronald up and down. Ronald sidled toward the door. Jorgensen grabbed an ax off the wall and held it with both hands across his chest.

"If I find out you've stolen some checks, it's going to be a very bad situation for you."

Confirmation Jorgensen was a geek. When you threaten somebody with an ax, you're supposed to say, "I'm going to chop your head off." Jorgensen scuttled sideways toward the desk. Ronald moved to keep the distance between them. "Have you been reading my poetry?" Jorgensen said. He sounded worried, not angry.

"Yes. The alliteration is alluring. Your rhymes are remarkable."

Jorgensen laid the ax on the desk. "You're the reporter from *The Eagle*, Ronald Truluck, aren't you? You came to my house." He laughed with relief. "It's good to see you again but what are you doing here?"

"I'm working on a story."

Jorgensen replaced the ax in its hanging spot. "A book review? A color piece? I'm a writer, you know."

"It's about Lamont Moody."

"No!" Jorgensen yelped like a textile machine had ripped his hand apart. He dropped into his chair and started scribbling on a legal pad as if Ronald wasn't there.

"How long have you been working for the city?"

Was it ethical for a reporter to trigger a person's emotional state and then take advantage of it to get better quotes? He'd decide later, depending on the quality of the quotes. Jorgensen slammed his pencil onto the desk so hard it bounced onto the floor.

"That, sir, is none of your business."

"If you don't tell me, I'll just ask the city manager."

"Do not invade my privacy!"

"You're a public employee, Bill. Your salary is public information."

Jorgensen stood and wheeled toward Ronald, his pasty face inflamed.

"Do not ask about that!" He advanced on Ronald. "I'm not afraid to act in a violent manner."

Ronald backed out of the building. He was willing to fight for the right to public records in court, but not in an equipment shed with a dirt floor. A pickup pulled up to the shed and two guys wearing city employee shirts began unloading a riding lawn mower.

"Do you guys work for Bill Jorgensen?" Ronald said.

"Hell no," said a wiry Black man with a goatee trimmed to a sharp point. "He checks the equipment in and out, or he's supposed to. But he's nobody's supervisor."

"Me either," said the other guy, a big headneck. "He just showed up one day and started doing the equipment list."

The men pushed the riding lawn mower into the shed and came out with two gas-powered push mowers and a metal gas can.

"Why you asking?" the headneck said.

"Can he hear us?" Ronald whispered.

"Naw. He snuck out the back door."

"I'm a reporter for *The Eagle*. I think there's something fishy about how Jorgensen got his job."

"There's something fishy about the way he *don't* do his job," the Black guy said. "He ain't here half the time. He's supposed to keep these written logs of when the equipment goes in and out, but we end up doing it most of the time, just like before he got hired."

"Does he ever cut grass or trim weeds?"

"He never lifts a finger," the Black guy said.

"Where does he go when he's not here?"

The men tied down the mowers in the truck bed with a neat arrangement of ropes.

"We don't know," the Black guy said. "He comes and goes. He's getting paid for doing nothing while we're working our butts off. It ain't right."

"What're your names? This is great stuff."

The men looked at each other. "Just call us King Arthur and Freddy Fat Ass," the Black guy said.

They drove away laughing, unquotable because Ronald didn't know their identities.

CHAPTER TWENTY-SIX

Ronald proposed *The Eagle* conduct an exclusive investigation of a do-nothing city employee who screwed around on the taxpayer's dime. He didn't mention the employee was Bill Jorgensen and that if the story worked, it might revive Lamontgate.

Mr. Carlton banged his pipe against an ashtray.

"I'm furious," he said. "This man is ripping off the public. He's cheating you and me. This is why our taxes are so high, because people like this layabout can get a high-paying job with the city and screw off all day. I want this story."

Ronald had never seen his boss so excited. The man didn't bat an eye when he heard about burglars stealing women's underwear or vandalizing churches, but cheating taxpayers was more than a crime. It was a sin—something Charles Manson would have done if he lived in Millerton.

"Can I skip my regular police beat stuff while I work on it?" Ronald said.

"Yes. This story is your priority now." He looked Ronald in the face. "There's an old saying that goes, 'The job of the newspaper is to comfort the afflicted and afflict the comfortable.' Well, that's what we're about to do, son. Heads are going to roll at city hall, and not just department supervisors. I'm talking about people on the city council. I can see Stick's fingerprints all over this catastrophe."

"This is outrageous!" Martha said. "What is this layabout's name?"

All eyes turned to Ronald. He'd been waiting for this moment. He unfolded his notebook and flipped through the pages as if searching for the name. "Bill Jorgensen," he said.

The newsroom went silent. No phones rang. Nobody touched their typewriter keys.

"Well," Mr. Carlton said. "That doesn't make one bit of difference. We'll write about Bill Jorgensen like he was anybody else. That means you've got to be solid. You've got to get everything on the record, like everything else we put in the paper. Don't go off half-cocked. Don't interview somebody without telling us. And just because Bill Jorgensen is screwing the city doesn't mean Lamont Moody did anything wrong. The two things aren't necessarily connected."

"Got it," Ronald said. "I'll be very careful."

Mr. Carlton was walking the line again. Telling Ronald to get to the bottom of things but sending the unspoken message that life would be better if he didn't stir things up. He wanted Ronald to fail.

"Before you do any reporting, go to the courthouse and spend a few hours in the clerk's office looking up this man's public records," Martha said. "Find out everything."

She returned to her desk, as if the conversation had been paused. Ronald was a step ahead.

"Already done," he said, tapping a folder of court papers. "William Roger Jorgensen, forty-three years old. Used to be married to Carlene Shelton, who was seven years older and divorced him on grounds of mental cruelty. The first wife moved to Texas with the two kids. Jorgensen's been married eight years to his current wife, Sarah, who's ten years older."

"He likes older women," Mr. Carlton observed.

"Legally, minor traffic violations and two car repossessions. It's not clear how he was making a living before he got this job with the city. He taught

English at the high school for a couple of years but got fired, according to Linda."

"My sister said he spent all day reciting his own poetry in class instead of teaching them how to write a simple sentence," Linda said.

Another mark against Jorgensen. He cheated children out of precious knowledge.

"We need to know more about his city job," Martha said. "How much he's paid, what his duties are. His job title. I want to see his job application."

Ronald described his encounter with Jorgensen while lunching with Shelly and Marcus at Burger King. They sat in their favorite booth facing the door, so they could watch people coming in and out.

"You should have taken the guy's checkbook," Marcus said. "Then you'd know how much money he's making from the city."

"That would be theft. Besides, the city manager will tell me his salary," Ronald said.

"They'll find a way to hide the information," Marcus said.

"He's right, the city will always lie to you. They're the government and the government is always trying to screw over the people and hide the truth," Shelly said. She took a ladylike nibble of a Whopper dripping with an orange sauce. She looked at Ronald and Marcus. "I've got an idea, if you two have the balls to do it."

"What's that?" Marcus said. He was offended a woman had referred to his testicles.

"You should follow Bill Jorgensen around and shoot photos of him screwing off on city time."

Clandestine activity like this was an unheard-of move for *The Eagle*. Half the paper's stories were born of press releases. But Shelly was right. Pictures would tell the story better than any wimpy document from city hall. There was precedent. Ronald had watched a *60 Minutes* segment that used a hidden camera.

"You're right. We'll do it," Ronald said. Marcus nodded consent.

"Does Jorgensen know what kind of car you drive?" Shelly said.

"I think he does. I drove it to Candler Park."

"You need a different car. Let's swap for a couple of days."

She took a key off her flower keychain and dropped it on the table between their trays. Ronald hesitated. This was not an even exchange. The Galaxie was like Ronald: unglamorous, but hardworking and dependable. Her stubby Chevy Nova was a collection of dents held together with liberal bumper stickers. The windshield wipers didn't work and neither did the fuel gauge. That's why she ran out of gas a couple of times a month while driving home from a night meeting of the county commission. Ronald had rescued her twice.

The next day, Ronald and Marcus slumped low into the front seat of the Nova so they could remain unseen while watching Jorgensen's yellow Vega parked outside the equipment shed.

"What's with this cloak and dagger crap?" Marcus said. "We're going to sneak around Millerton all day? Why don't I just walk up to him and take his damn picture."

"If Jorgensen knows we're watching, he won't screw off."

"I didn't sign up for this kind of assignment. Have you seen my portfolio?" Marcus was talented and egotistical. He was always showing off shots of his girlfriend and shadowy still lifes of old houses. "Walker Evans or Gordon Parks wouldn't be caught dead shooting this kind of crap."

"They're unavailable, so we're forced to use you."

After an hour, Jorgensen came out and drove around town for an hour, using many of the routes Ronald employed when he was killing time. He stopped at Burnette's Pond, a county park, where he sat on a stump writing on his legal pad. Marcus crept behind a stand of trees and photographed Jorgensen at work.

"I got the shot," Marcus said when he returned to the car. "Let's go back to the office."

"We need more pictures. We need full documentation," Ronald said.

They sat for two hours, watching Jorgensen write. Ronald didn't know if Marcus smoked pot, but he took a chance and pulled out a thin joint. They smoked and made jokes about their coworkers at *The Eagle*. Jorgensen got into the Vega and drove to Lake Miller, where he sat at a picnic table writing when he wasn't staring at the water. Marcus sauntered along the shoreline, pretending to take pictures of frogs and tadpoles while shooting Jorgensen.

"This is stupid," Marcus said when he got back to the car.

"This is journalism. It's not always glamorous."

They followed Jorgensen to the 7-Eleven on the bypass where he bought gas and looked at girlie magazines for twenty minutes. Then Jorgensen drove home. Back at the newsroom, Ronald sat down with Martha and Mr. Carlton and explained how he, with an assist from Marcus, documented Jorgensen's malfeasance.

"You stalked Bill Jorgensen and took pictures without him knowing?" Mr. Carlton said. "The man may be doing something wrong but that doesn't mean we do something wrong. That's not how we gather news. Who in the hell decided to do that?"

Ronald and Marcus shrunk in their chairs. Ronald, unlike Marcus, knew Mr. Carlton's anger was short-lived.

"Marcus and I decided to take the initiative," Ronald said, leaving Shelly out of the decision. "And I'm glad we did, because the situation is much worse than we imagined."

That stopped the editor's anger. "Worse? How could it be worse?"

"Jorgensen went to the 7-Eleven and looked at pornographic magazines on the city's dime."

Penthouse and *Playboy* didn't qualify as pornography to Ronald, but he knew Mr. Carlton and Martha would think they did.

"He's looking at pornography while getting paid by the city? Unbelievable," Martha said. "I know the secret photographs are an unorthodox step, but we've got to do something to stop this. I mean, pornography, I.J."

"What an immoral, incompetent screw-off," Mr. Carlton said, swayed by Martha's outrage. "Jorgensen doesn't know better than to cheat the taxpayer right out in the open. I want this story as soon as possible."

CHAPTER
TWENTY-SEVEN

Ronald got up early and drove to Shelly's house to trade cars. She invited him inside and he drank coffee, smoked, and read newspapers at the kitchen table with her and Steve for an hour. They subscribed to three papers. Their utility room was crammed with stacks of old papers as well as a trash can heaping with empty beer cans. Steve was working on a story about an assistant DA who pressured women defendants into having sex with him in his office. Shelly was profiling a deputy who owned five three-legged dogs. Ronald was still chasing Lamont through Bill Jorgensen.

He drove back to Millerton and sat in his Galaxie near the equipment shed for thirty minutes. No Jorgensen. He drove to the library and found the Vega. Meg, the assistant librarian, waved from behind the checkout desk. He'd interviewed her for a story about a summer reading program.

"Are you going to interview Bill Jorgensen?" she said.

How did she know? Was he that obvious?

"Sure, sooner or later."

"I can't wait for his new book of poetry to come out. It's going to be better than his first one."

Martha and Monica had mentioned Jorgensen wrote poetry, and Jorgensen himself said he was a writer during their terse interview in the equipment shed. But a lot of people said they wrote poetry.

"I love his poetry. It's confessional, romantic, heartfelt." Meg grabbed a thin book with a red cover off a shelf behind her and laid it on the desk. "This is his first one. You can borrow it."

He peeked into the periodicals room where Jorgensen sat writing on a legal pad and took the book to a study carrel on the other side of the library. *Whispers of My Soul* was forty-four pages long. Part One was the internal monologue of a lovestruck young man who wanted to kiss a woman who was beautiful in her own, peculiar way nobody else noticed. He used lots of alliteration about lonely, lingering love. The sex was implied.

Part Two was written by the same man, a bit older, who'd been dumped by the beautiful woman from Part One. She was materialistic and shallow and not very nice. He dreamed of stabbing her to death and killing himself but didn't because that would make his kids orphans. "I dropped the blade, accepting the fate I could not evade," the poem concluded.

The cover was devoid of a title or other words. The edges of the pages were ragged. It didn't have a copyright symbol, a title page, a table of contents, or any features he'd noticed in real books. It was self-published, a description one of his professors had uttered in condescension about a fellow professor's book. Jorgensen's book did have a ten-sentence entry on the About the Author page, starting with where he was born and ending with his three favorite poets—William Blake, John Donne, and Rod McKuen. A throat cleared. Bill Jorgensen stood in a faded denim shirt, holding his legal pad across his chest.

"Meg said you wanted to talk. About my book," he said.

Two days ago, Jorgensen waved an ax at Ronald in the equipment shed. Now he stood waiting, showing respect, because he wanted to be interviewed. The power of the press was real.

"Sit down," Ronald said.

"But no questions about Lamont Moody."

"If I ask a question you don't like, then don't answer it."

Jorgensen didn't move, weighing suspicion against his desire for acclaim. Ronald knew a writer's ego—even his own ego about cop briefs—was beyond logic.

"Your poems are interesting," Ronald said. Not a lie.

"Okay, but nothing about Mr. Moody." Jorgensen pulled a chair up to the carrel. Up close, he emanated poor health with his dry skin and yellowing, cracked fingernails.

"First a few biographical questions," Ronald said and Jorgensen was off and running. He sped through his life—parents, college, writing press releases in the army—and was starting to describe the obstacles he'd overcome to write poetry when Ronald interrupted.

"What do you do for the city?" he said.

"Why is that important?"

"Because I write for *The Eagle.* We cover Millerton."

"That's irrelevant because the story's about my book, not my job. And your story will appear in the Associated Press, won't it? It's a national story, don't you think?"

"If it's a good story, the AP will pick it up." The AP operated in a distant galaxy. Ronald had no idea how the AP got its stories. "A poet who works a nine-to-five job, that sounds like an enticing angle to me."

"If you say so," Jorgensen said. "My title is recreation department lawn maintenance equipment supervisor. I supervise three people, though there's one vacancy."

"Why is there a vacancy?"

"If you must know, Joey Burris got thrown in jail. The police say he broke into the elementary school and stole ice cream from the kitchen freezer. They found Joey with chocolate smeared all over his mouth for God's sake."

"Police Put Ice-Cream Bandit in Cooler," read the headline on Ronald's cop brief.

"That's a good example of the kind of people I work with," Jorgensen said. "They're unable to see how satisfying their temporary desires might not be a good idea in the long term. To people like Joey, delayed gratification is an alien concept. He couldn't understand the idea if I spent five hours explaining it to him."

"Who else do you supervise? I talked to two guys outside the shop."

"Let's talk about my new book now."

"Fine. It's poetry again, right?"

"That's my métier," Jorgensen said. "I've been drawn to verse since my school days. My style is evolving, as you'll see. These new poems are in free verse."

Ronald shaped an amazed O with his mouth.

"Does your wife like your poetry?"

"She's not much of a reader, except for seed packages. She's a good country girl and doesn't get caught up in anything fancy like poetry."

Maybe that's why he didn't mention her on the About the Author page.

"These poems"—Ronald tapped *Whispers of My Soul*—"are very personal. Are they autobiographical?"

"All literature is autobiographical. Any writer would tell you that. A writer must base his work on his life, on his ..."

"You stabbed somebody?"

"That's imaginary. Nothing like that has happened in my real life."

"Don't get me wrong; the stabbing poem is my favorite thing in the whole book. It's not realistic, but it sounds like you meant it. The blood and everything."

"It didn't happen. Even the poem says it didn't happen. It was just something he thought about doing, but he didn't."

"Who's 'he?' You?"

"No, not me. It's a fictional narrator. He doesn't exist. You can't call him on the phone. The narrator represents every frustrated man who has ever had a disagreement with a member of the opposite sex. Let's just say he represents all mankind."

Ronald wrote "all mankind" in his notepad.

"I get it; it's all in your mind. But who did the narrator imagine they were stabbing? Your first wife? Because it sounds like you don't like her much."

"I'm not talking about *Whispers* anymore. It's ancient history. Let's talk about my new book. It's called *My Life in Limbo*."

"Catchy title. What's it about?"

"The tricks people play on themselves, the self-deceptions and compromises we're all guilty of. Every poem examines a different person's psyche and captures their life and their speech cadences and their loves and hates and dreams and failures. And I guess you could say it's about people waiting for something to happen that will alter the course of their life."

"Any more stabbing poems?"

"No more of those. *My Life in Limbo* should be published in about three months. I'll make sure you get a review copy. I promise. What about the photograph?"

"What do you have in mind?"

"A picture of me sitting on a big rock at sunset, with half my face in shadow."

"Could we shoot it at your house? At your writing desk?"

"That won't work. My wife doesn't like to let strangers inside."

"I'll get back to you," Ronald said. *The Eagle* already had plenty of pictures of Jorgensen.

The poet said he had to go. Ronald still had Lamont questions and walked Jorgensen to his Vega. This was the moment to end it. With luck, Ronald would never speak again to the alliterating loser.

"How long do you expect to work in your city job?" Ronald said. "The job Lamont Moody gave you so you'd keep your mouth shut about his wreck."

"You said you wouldn't ask any questions about Mr. Moody. You gave your word. You lied to me. Who told you Lamont got me the job?"

"A confidential source. Did you apply at city hall? Fill out an application? Submit a résumé that says you're a published poet who doesn't know one thing about lawn mowers?"

Jorgensen backed up against the side of his Vega.

"Mr. Moody said he'd take care of things. I didn't have to go through the application process." Jorgensen looked around the parking lot as if a rescuer might be nearby. "He said it happened all the time. I just showed up one day and I've been doing it ever since. It's all legal."

The incriminating quote. "It's all legal" was almost as good as Nixon's "I am not a crook."

"But you don't do the job, do you? You leave the equipment shed for hours at a time. Two guys I talked to said you were not in the equipment shed very often. I've followed you."

"What in the world are you talking about?"

"Where you went, I went. You went to the lake to scribble. You went to the 7-Eleven on the bypass and looked at dirty magazines."

"Only on my lunch break. I needed a change of scenery to write."

"I bet you've spent twenty hours in the library reading room this week."

"It was two and a half hours three days ago. Meg will tell you."

"Why weren't you working? Why are you cheating the taxpayers?"

"I'm not cheating anybody. You'll hear from my lawyer!"

Jorgensen got in the Vega, but it stalled out. Ronald and another guy gave him a push to get the car moving, then he returned *Whispers of My Soul* to Meg at the front desk.

"You've already read it?" she said.

"I didn't need to. Bill told me everything I needed to know."

CHAPTER
TWENTY-EIGHT

It was noon. Ronald was ready to write, but he knew Mr. Carlton and Martha would ask him to interview one more source, run down another document. He needed to get the story written before they could deny the invincible righteousness of his prose.

He flew up the newsroom stairs two at a time and went straight to his desk, ignoring greetings from Linda and Snap. He rolled copy paper into the typewriter. He lit a cigarette and dropped his fingertips to the typewriter keys. The words traveled from his brain to the paper, his fingers a conduit. No sentence fragments. No starting and stopping.

"Using covert surveillance, *The Eagle* has documented how a City of Millerton recreation department supervisor visited the public library, scribbled poetry at a city park, and drove around aimlessly while still earning a taxpayer-funded paycheck."

But the second sentence didn't flow. It didn't even leak. He could go in a dozen directions, but which one? He lightly touched the typewriter keys, praying the typewriter would take control and move his fingers in the right direction. Maybe his lead wasn't very good. Maybe he didn't have the instincts. Maybe Ronald, at the core of his being, was a failure.

His newsroom colleagues merrily slammed their typewriters, except for Martha. She inspected him across the room with unforgiving eyes. He couldn't look away. She knew he was paralyzed with indecision. She knew he'd never write the story. Her phone rang. She picked it up and said, "Hi, Mother." This would be a long conversation, at least ten minutes, giving him time to get back on track. Marcus, unaware of Ronald's creative crisis, dropped half a dozen glossy black-and-white photos on his desk.

"I think these are pretty good, considering I had to sneak up on the guy," Marcus said. "But keep in mind, this is not what I'm doing the rest of my journalistic career. I'm into portraits of people, important people, and regular people. Pictures that mean something. But these are okay."

The photographs captured Jorgensen writing at the parks. They were in focus and told the story. Ronald picked up one and held it in front of his face, as if the image would ignite an idea. It showed Jorgensen pulling his lower lip with his fingertips while staring into space. He looked like Ronald felt. Indecisive. Unfocused. Weak. Laughable. Ronald attacked the typewriter anew.

"A Millerton recreation department employee has spent many hours sharpening his verse when he should have been sharpening lawn mower blades. In an interview with *The Eagle*, Bill Jorgensen said his title is lawn maintenance equipment supervisor. He was hired to oversee the crew that cuts grass and picks up trash at the city parks.

"But this *Eagle* reporter and a staff photographer, working undercover, observed Jorgensen ignoring his official duties and instead spending hours writing poetry at various locations throughout the city, such as the Miller County Public Library and Burnette's Pond County Park, all while being paid a salary by city taxpayers.

"Jorgensen declined to comment about why he chose to cheat the city's taxpayers, but admitted spending at least two and a half hours in the library reading room earlier this week.

"The former high school teacher said he was working on poems for his second book of verse, *My Life in Limbo*. He published his first book of poetry, *Whispers of My Soul*, two years ago.

"Jorgensen said he didn't go through the normal city hiring process but was placed in the job by city council member Lamont Moody. 'It's all legal,' Jorgensen said, without offering further explanation."

Martha hung up the phone and rubbed her temples. She circled behind Ronald to read his copy, the witch hazel in her hairspray tickling his nose.

"This has a lot of holes. Craters. You need to mention the pornography in the second paragraph. How much money does the city pay him?" she said.

"I'll find out tomorrow. I've accomplished the hard part. I documented he's not working. He confessed when he said, 'It's all legal.'"

"Maybe it is legal. What was the start date on the job?"

"I'll get that too. Why are you nitpicking? Aren't you outraged?"

"You're what, twenty-four years old? What do you know about outrage?"

"I'm twenty-two. How old are you?"

Martha paced to avoid the question. Shelly crept up to his desk, her face pink with alarm. "Is somebody in trouble?" she asked. She was worried because she had so many corrections.

"Bill Jorgensen, maybe," Martha said.

"Bill Jorgensen, for sure," Ronald said.

"And he's a poet?" Shelly lifted her aviator glasses to sit on top of her head. "Are you sure you want to destroy a poet? That's cruel—like killing a mockingbird."

"But his poems aren't very good," Ronald said.

"Poetry is very important, Ronald. We need poets more than we need reporters. They explain things normal people can't. I write poetry."

Marcus called out, "I'd love to hear one of your poems, Shelly."

"Well, okay. This one ran in the college literary magazine."

"Cool it," Ronald said. "We're talking about my story, not your poetry."

Martha said, "I think it's a fine time to hear a poem. Shelly, go ahead."

"I agree," said Linda, joining the group.

Shelly straightened her shoulders. Ronald saw the earnest sixth-grader who won the good citizenship award before turning hippie. Shelly said, "It's called 'The Flowers of Death.'"

On his casket I lay the flowers,
As sunset peeked through the rosewood bower.
His flag-draped casket was lowered into the ground
But I could not watch, I did not look down.
His weeping mother clasped my hand
And said, "We'll see him some day in the promised land."
I did not tell her I disbelieved in her savior
Because this was her moment of grief to savor.
We walked away puffing small clouds with our breaths
Leaving behind his memory and the flowers of death.

"I didn't know your boyfriend was killed in Vietnam," Linda said while hugging Shelly. "I'm so sorry."

"He wasn't. But my high school best friend's brother was and I went to the funeral. That was the inspiration for the poem. Did you like it?"

"I loved it," Linda said.

"How'd you like it, Ronald?" Shelly said.

"It rhymes, unlike Bill Jorgensen's pathetic poetry."

"He's trying. That's what counts."

"The quality of his poems is beside the point. He's cheating the taxpayers. That's an immoral, unforgivable crime." You could never go wrong attacking people who cheated the taxpayers.

"It's immoral to silence a poet—any poet," Shelly said and stalked to the bathroom.

"What does Lamont say about helping Jorgensen get a job with the city?" Martha said.

"I didn't ask," Ronald said. "At the time, I didn't know he'd pulled strings to get Jorgensen hired."

"You've got to get a response from Lamont and the city manager. And the mayor."

"Lamont won't talk to me. He's got this guy named Turkey who would love to kill me."

Martha solidified her stance. She put her hands on her hips. Ronald had no chance.

CHAPTER
TWENTY-NINE

He called Lamont's office, hoping for a quick no comment. Then he could say he'd done his best to get both sides of the story.

"He won't talk with you. Ever," Lamont's secretary said.

"I need to ask one question. I'll give you the question and then you can ask Lamont and he can formulate his answer and call me back. No surprises. Do you have a pen and paper?"

Dial tone. A hang-up was not the same as a no comment. Ronald had not done his journalistic duty. He needed to find Lamont in the flesh.

He went to the Millerton Diner for a sandwich and found Lamont at a back table with Mayor Stick.

"Still bird-dogging me, aren't you?" Lamont said, lounging with his belly exposed to the world. Stick mumbled a hello, his hands encircling a plastic iced-tea glass. He was a classic ectomorph, dressed today in golf shirt and beltless slacks.

"Okay if I join you?" Ronald said.

Nobody said yes and nobody said no. He asked to borrow a chair from the next table where a man in work clothes held a hamburger with both hands. The man said his son-in-law was supposed to be there thirty minutes ago but hadn't shown up, so why the hell not. Ronald slipped in between Lamont and Stick. Two plates with sandwich crusts rested on the table.

"You're pushy," Lamont grunted.

"That's how reporters do their job," said Stick, a surprise ally. Ronald squelched the idea of asking him about his daughter's affair with Dwight Bennett.

"I interviewed Bill Jorgensen," Ronald said. "He said you got him the job with the recreation department."

"Maybe I did, maybe I didn't. I do know the man. You can quote me on that."

"But he ducks out of work all the time," Ronald said. "I followed Jorgensen, and he spent hours away from the equipment hut."

"He's doing what?" Stick said, sitting up straighter.

"He's not putting in his eight hours a day. He goes to the lake, the library, and the convenience store. He drives around killing time. I interviewed him at the library, and he admitted spending two and a half hours in the reading room."

"Who made you a police officer?" Lamont said.

"I need a comment. Jorgensen said you told him it was all perfectly legal."

Jorgensen never used the word "perfectly" in describing anything. He said the hiring process was legal, not his avoidance of work. Exactitude was unimportant. Lamont was unnerved.

"Wait a minute," Lamont said. "Maybe Jorgensen was doing repair work at the library. We need to keep city facilities in working order to avoid injuries to citizens. A big lawsuit could kill us." He turned to Stick. "Kill us!"

"What *was* this Jorgensen fellow doing in the reading room?" Stick said. "Reading?"

"He was writing poetry."

Silence settled over the table.

"Poetry?" Stick said. "What kind of poetry?"

"Free verse," Ronald said. "Poetry that doesn't rhyme."

Revulsion filled Stick's face.

"Then it's not poetry," he declared. Pivoting to Lamont he said, "You told me we needed somebody in the equipment shed, but this screw-off is still on city payroll and writing poetry? What's going on, Lamont?"

"Stick, Stick, hold on," Lamont said. His flushed cheeks were potted with massive pores. "One of the guys on Jorgensen's work crew quit on him out of the blue. Bill may have stayed on to take up the slack until we fill that position."

Lamont settled back into his normal sitting position. Mayor Stick said, "We do need to keep the parks mowed and trimmed and the trash picked up. That was one of my campaign issues, you know."

Stick blew with the wind. Mr. Carlton called him Twig. Ronald could sway him.

"But nobody 'quit' Jorgensen's crew," Ronald said. "Joey Burris got arrested when he broke into the elementary school kitchen. The police found him with ice cream smeared all over his face."

"That was Joey?" Stick said. "I hadn't heard that."

Stick chortled. Ronald had flipped the conversation into two against one.

"And Lamont's lying about Jorgensen's duties. He doesn't fix anything. He checks equipment in and out, but the guys say they don't need him to do it. He's not around three-quarters of the time."

"His men said that?" Stick said.

Ronald nodded. Stick drained his tea. "I don't like the sound of this, Lamont."

A waitress just out of high school walked up with an iced-tea pitcher and said, "Anybody need a refill?"

"Stick, Stick, Stick, Ronald here hates my guts," Lamont said. "I don't know why. Maybe because I work hard and believe in the principles of free enterprise. But he doesn't."

The waitress backed away. Lamont had almost called Ronald a communist.

Stick said to Ronald, "Well, do you? Believe in free enterprise?"

Ronald had discussed this issue with friends in college. Their conclusion: No nation with a state-run economy had ever produced a decent rock song. If that made Ronald a capitalist, so be it.

"I believe in freedom," Ronald said. "Including freedom of the press."

"Quit dancing around, you lousy pinko," Lamont said.

"Did you give Bill Jorgensen that job by circumventing standard hiring procedures?" Ronald leaned toward Lamont. "Because that's what he told me."

"None of your damn business."

People at surrounding tables stopped eating to observe the argument.

"I'm making it my business," Ronald said. "I'm not standing still while the honest, hardworking, church-going people of Millerton are fleeced and cheated and ripped off and taken advantage of by Lamont Moody's starry-eyed poet who won't put in an honest day's work ..."

"A poet?" said the man who let Ronald borrow the chair. "You mean like Shakespeare?"

Ronald, winded from his declaration, nodded.

"That's right, the city's got a poet on the payroll," Stick said, standing up. "And this reporter and I are going down to city hall to get to the bottom of this thing and pronto. This situation is wrong as rain."

"Wait a minute," Lamont said, but Stick and Ronald were already walking out.

"Go get 'em, Stick," said the chair loaner, and laid a potato chip on his extended tongue.

CHAPTER THIRTY

Ronald followed the mayor in his car to city hall. The two of them marched down waxed linoleum corridors and stepped into an office to find Dot Smith, the secretary to city manager Danny Tarlton, sitting at her desk with an apple lifted halfway to her mouth.

"Hello, Stick," she said, laying the apple on a paper towel and touching the corner of her lips with a fingertip. "I didn't know you'd be dropping by."

"Sorry to interrupt your lunch, Dot."

"That's fine." Dot was renowned for her niceness.

"I'm trying to help this reporter," Stick said. "You know Ronald, don't you?"

Ronald and Dot said their hellos, having interacted a few times. She'd just gotten a divorce, according to Martha, which explained Dot's new hairstyle and updated look: teal turtleneck and plaid bell-bottoms.

"Is Danny here?" Stick said. "I need him to look up some information."

"He's not, but maybe I can help you. What is it you need?"

"The paperwork on the hiring for Bill Jorgensen."

Dot flipped through a file cabinet drawer and handed a folder to Stick. He opened the door to Danny's inner office and walked inside. Ronald and Dot looked at each other in disbelief. For Stick to stroll into Danny's office was a violation of city hall protocol. Stick, the city's highest elected official, had lucked into office when the previous mayor decided not to run at the last minute. Nobody respected Stick. Danny, though a city employee who answered to Stick, ruled through competence and likability. Danny had more clout than Stick. Everybody in town knew that except Stick.

Ronald followed Stick into the office, carried by his need to know. They sat down at a round table. Stick opened the file. It contained one piece of paper.

Bill Jorgensen's résumé said that besides teaching English, he worked two years selling Amway and eight years as a freelance writer. That was the same as saying he was unemployed. He'd published one book of poetry and his hobbies were seventeenth-century British literature, chess, and charcoal sketching.

"What a loser," Stick said. "Nobody makes any money selling Amway."

"How'd he get hired?" Ronald said.

Stick puffed his cheeks and exhaled.

"Lamont sold us a bill of goods. He said the city needed somebody to keep an eye on the equipment shed because a push mower and a trimmer and some other tools went missing. I needed his vote to raise the business license fee, so I said fine, let's do it. I took Lamont's word that the man was honest."

"Can you give me the minutes of the meeting when he was hired?"

"Nope. We just talked in an executive session and decided to do it."

The scandal was worse than Ronald imagined. The mayor and council disregarded the principles of good government. They should have voted on the hiring in open session.

Somebody said something in the outer room. Danny Tarlton stepped into the office. His office.

"Stick, what are you doing in here? Ronald?" Though smiling, Danny looked heavier, paler, and unhealthier than ever. Maybe being hated by Stick was taking a toll on him.

"We're getting to the bottom of some shit, that's what we're doing," Stick said. "It's about Bill Jorgensen. Ronald here says he's screwing off all the time. When he's supposed to be working, he's out writing poetry for free."

"He means free verse," Ronald corrected. "It doesn't rhyme."

"Why would he do that?" Danny said.

"It doesn't matter why," Stick said. "The question is how you could let it happen?"

A fight was about to break out and Ronald was caught in the crossfire. Danny's facial muscles surrendered to the laws of gravity. His smile disappeared. He assumed the power position behind his desk, the leather chair creaking when he sat.

"Calm down, Stick," Danny said. "I didn't want to give Jorgensen that job. You and Lamont did, so don't blame me."

"It's your job to make sure city employees don't rip off the taxpayers."

"Let's talk about that later, not in front of a reporter," Danny said. "Okay?"

Stick took off his wristwatch and wound it, like he didn't have anything better to do. It was a cowardly move. He'd backed down but was pretending he'd lost interest in attacking. Danny said to Ronald, "What do you need?"

"A copy of Jorgensen's résumé, his job application, his pay information, his job description, his title, and the executive session minutes from the meeting when he was hired."

"You hear that, Dot?" Danny called out.

"Got it," she said.

"And I need a comment about Jorgensen," Ronald said.

"I'll comment for the city," Stick said and put his watch back on. "I'm the mayor."

"I'll take both your comments," Ronald said. He couldn't afford to alienate Danny, the more valuable source. Stick was always a good bet to say something dumb and therefore newsworthy.

Danny spun a coherent statement denying knowledge of anything wrong, promised to fix the Jorgensen problem, and proclaimed that

Millerton was founded on the principle of an honest day's work for an honest day's pay.

"Open a window," Stick said. "I'm about to pass out from the smell of bullshit."

Stick unleashed a stream-of-consciousness rant that connected Lamont Moody, North Vietnam, North Carolina, the Soviet Union, Watergate, fluoridation, and Ted Kennedy. Stick was a good argument against representative democracy.

When Stick stopped, he and Ronald left city hall. In the parking lot, Stick started babbling again. Ronald had been raised to always respect adults, but this time he walked away.

CHAPTER
THIRTY-ONE

Ronald was writing his story again when Danny came into the newsroom beaming like he was stepping onto a stage. The city manager went from desk to desk shaking hands and making small talk. His gut jiggled when he laughed. Shelly gave him a cursory greeting because Danny gave her the creeps. Danny disengaged from his fans and laid a manila folder on Ronald's desk. Martha came over to look.

"Here's the stuff you asked for, plus an invoice," Danny said. "I guess he did a decent job inventorying the equipment shed because we found out there wasn't as much stuff missing as we thought. We paid him four hundred dollars for two week's work, then his contract ended. Are you sure he was still working out of the Candler Park shed? We're not paying him anymore."

Ronald looked at the papers in the folder. "I saw him there a few days ago and he had a desk set up like he spent a lot of time there. He kept a checkbook in a drawer. He had a nameplate on the desk. Why would he go into work if the city's not paying him?"

"It's weird, but I met Bill Jorgensen once and he's a weird guy."

"So, he hasn't been cheating the city out of any money," Ronald said, "because you're not paying him now, is that what you're saying? Are you one hundred percent sure he's not getting paid?"

Asking questions in an angry tone of voice was a more dignified tactic than laying his head on the desk and crying. The story had vanished. He had made a mistake.

"I'm sure. It's still a problem for the city because there's a liability factor," Danny said. "I mean, what if Jorgensen cuts his hand off with a chainsaw owned by the city? Not only would the city have to pay out a lot of money, but he'd never be able to write poetry again."

Everybody cackled except Ronald and Martha. They traded morose looks.

"I've got to have an unpleasant meeting with the top folks in the recreation department," Danny said. "They didn't know Jorgensen was hanging out on city property, and that's a problem. Thanks for bringing this to my attention, Ronald. I can't wait to read your story."

Ronald tried to follow Danny out of the office, but Martha blocked the door.

"What happened?" she said. "How did you get this so wrong? Bill Jorgensen wasn't cheating the city; he was giving the city free labor. Didn't you ask him about that?"

"When I interviewed him, he was evasive."

"Why didn't you go to Danny for the payment records first? If you had, you'd have known there wasn't a story. You wouldn't have stalked Jorgensen all over town, made Marcus shoot photographs in secret, confronted Bill Jorgensen with false accusations, and promised I.J. and me an investigative story that would win a state press association award. If Danny hadn't provided this information, we could have run a story that slandered Bill Jorgensen to kingdom come."

"I think you mean we would have libeled him because it would be written. Slander is a false spoken statement."

"I know the difference. When I.J. gets back to the office, he and I are going to discuss your future with *The Eagle.*"

"But I didn't make a mistake—not one that got in print. I just came close."

He was still on probation. They'd have good cause to let him go. Could he live down being fired by The Eaglet?

"When Danny and Dot tell everybody what happened, we'll be the laughingstock of city hall," Martha said. "Of the entire city."

He wouldn't endure being judged by the tiny minds of Millerton, with their grudges and feuds and whisper campaigns. Waiting to be fired was not an option.

"I don't give a damn what Danny and Dotty think. Screw them, screw *The Eagle*, and screw you. I resign, effective this moment. Now step aside."

She didn't try to stop him from walking out the door. Ronald drove around on autopilot and found himself parking in Monica's driveway. She answered the door with uncombed hair, looking like she'd been lying around watching TV in the middle of the day.

"What are you doing here?" she said. "Why didn't you call first? You can't just show up at my house."

"I'm here because I need to tell you something. Bill Jorgensen didn't have a do-nothing job with the city. He had a do-something job for a while, and then he kept going to work for some reason even though he wasn't getting paid. What I'm saying is I look dumb. There's no story. I just quit my job."

"That's a rash thing to do."

Her response was paltry, uncaring. His career, his personhood, was evaporating and she didn't recognize her culpability.

"It happened because you gave me a shitty tip," he said.

Monica pulled the door shut and stepped onto the porch. Ronald wasn't going to be invited inside for a glass of wine.

"Excuse me," she said. "I gave you that tip because you were floundering. Your story was going nowhere. I told you what Bill told me. It was your job to find out if it was true or not. Did you expect me to go out with a notepad and ask questions for you?"

She had a point. He was the journalist, not her. But Ronald was tired of admitting he'd made a mistake. He needed to do something decisive, even if it was the wrong thing.

"I'll carry your memory with me always, Monica," he said. "I wish you well in the future."

"Are *you* breaking up with *me*? On my doorstep in the middle of the day? Using some line you heard in a romantic movie? Let me show you how to break up with somebody, Ronald. If I see you walking down the street, I'm going to shut my eyes even if I'm driving in heavy traffic because I can't stand the sight of you. I'm going to burn the sheets on my bed. I hope your ugly car runs off the road and drops into the river and you never come up for air. I'm going to have brain surgery to wipe you out of my memory."

She really knew how to break up. Ronald got behind the wheel of the Galaxie. Before he turned the key, Monica's inflamed face appeared at the window. He rolled it down half an inch.

"You don't understand *The Great Gatsby* worth a shit!" she shouted and marched back into her house.

CHAPTER
THIRTY-TWO

Bill Jorgensen couldn't be found at the equipment shed, the library, or his other haunts. Ronald parked in front of his house on Archdale Street. No yellow Vega in the driveway. Sarah Jorgensen was dressed up when she opened the door. Her hair hung to her shoulders, and she wore lipstick, a green-and-yellow dress with a belt, and brown shoes with low heels. Perfume, even.

"We're not talking," she said.

"I'm looking for your worthless husband. I want to know why he's been going to the equipment shed at Candler Park when the city's not paying him one red cent."

"Not been paid? Come in."

Ronald stepped into a plain but neat living room. No reading material in sight, except *TV Guide* on the coffee table. She snapped off the television set and they sat on opposite ends of a sofa.

"Who told you Bill's not getting paid?" she said.

"Danny Tarlton."

"Who's he?"

How could she not know that? Danny was omnipresent in *The Eagle*.

"The city manager."

"Oh, he's some kind of big shot." She glared, wrinkles deepening by the second. "I think you've got your facts wrong."

"Look, lady, I'm a professional journalist. My facts are solid."

"Bill has money these days. In fact, he's taking me out to eat at a restaurant tonight for our anniversary. Why in the world would a man go to work if he's not getting paid?"

"That's what I came here to find out. I do know your husband isn't 'working' very much. He goes to the lake and the library and writes poetry in a legal pad."

"Poetry," she squawked. "He's doing that again? He already made a book about his poems a few years ago. Did you know that? It was about his first wife. I said, 'How much did you get paid for this book?' Thinking I might get a new car out of it, or a trip out of town. And you know what he said? Nothing. He paid somebody to get the thing printed. He spent money when he should have been making money."

"Bill's about to publish a second book of poetry."

"My God. You're kidding me."

"It's called *My Life in Limbo*."

"You mean like doing a dance under a stick?"

"It means you're stuck between two things, like heaven and hell."

"I'm going to give him hell, I can tell you that."

On cue, a car pulled into the driveway and rattled to a halt. Sarah padded to the screen door and waited while Ronald stood by the sofa. Bill Jorgensen stepped into his castle, wearing a plaid shirt.

"Don't you look nice," he said, then noticed Ronald. "Get the hell out of my house."

"Stay right where you are," Sarah said to Ronald, her eyes on fire.

"Get out," Bill said.

"Don't move," Sarah said. "The mortgage is in my name, not his. He can't tell you to get out of my house."

Ronald stayed put, but he felt like he might end up writing a cop brief about himself. She squared up in her going-out dress and said, "How much are you paying to get this limbo book published?"

Bill glared at Ronald. Did he think his wife would never find out?

"Never mind, Sarah. It doesn't matter."

"I do mind," she said and turned her head to Ronald. "You want to know why? After I found out Bill paid our good money to get that first book printed, money I earned cleaning bedpans at the nursing home, me and him had a come-to-Jesus meeting, didn't we, Bill?"

"I refuse to participate in this travesty," Bill said, but he didn't move.

"I said you can read poetry in your spare time, but you're not spending any more money on it. You're not buying poetry magazines and you're not spending one penny on getting something published in a book."

Bill shook his head and whispered "No, no, no," like that might shut up Sarah. Ronald saw a new story: Woman seeks divorce on grounds of poetry.

"And Bill whined and he pouted, but he knew he didn't have any place to go, because his mama wasn't speaking to him at the time. He promised me he'd do it. He'd give up his poetry dream and find a real job and help support this household."

"What a ludicrous assertion," Bill said.

"And he did get some jobs, but he lost 'em. Teaching English, the convenience store, a landscaping job, tutoring rich kids. Bill's better at getting fired than getting hired. And then Bill lucked up and got this job with the city that Mr. Lamont Moody helped him get. I thought, now he'll pull his weight. And I find out he's been telling me lies the whole time."

"You can be so small-minded," Bill said. "Mother was right about you."

"How much are you paying to get the book published?" she demanded, returning to the dollars-and-cents argument he'd never win. "Spit it out."

"If you must know, around three hundred dollars."

Ronald calculated. At twenty bucks an ounce, he could buy fifteen bags of decent Mexican reefer—more if he bought in bulk. Sarah had a different wish list.

"Good God, the bathroom floor is so rotten the commode wobbles and you're spending three hundred dollars on poems? When are you going to start living in the real world?"

"It's going to be published in a few months," Bill said. "By a small printing company a friend of mine runs in Winston-Salem. Sarah, I want to tell you something I hope will assuage your anger. I'm dedicating *My Life in Limbo* to my loving wife, Sarah Duncan Gottfried Jorgensen."

"Where in the tarnation is this three hundred dollars coming from? This reporter says you're not on the city payroll anymore. That you're working for free."

Bill shut his eyes tight, as if wishing himself to another dimension. He snapped them open and performed his own eye-drilling routine on Sarah.

"Okay, I fibbed about the job," Bill shouted. "Big deal. Are you happy now?"

"You were about to take me out to a restaurant for supper, so I know you've got money in your pocket. You know how much I make at the nursing home. You know how much I've got in my bank account, how much I spend on my arthritis medicine, how much I spent on gasoline for the lawnmower. I've not kept any secrets from you. How much have you got?"

How much? The eternal question.

"If you have to know, I've got one hundred and twenty-two dollars in my wallet," he said. "Mother's been sending me $400 a month. Aunt Mary died, and she put Mother in her will, and Mother is sharing the money with me."

"How come I never see this money come in the mail?" Sarah said. "Your mother hasn't sent me a birthday card in three years."

"It comes to a mailbox I keep at the post office," Jorgensen said.

"Oh ho," Sarah sang out. "I didn't know about that either. You've got a secret mailbox so you can get secret checks and dirty magazines with pictures of naked girls not wearing bras or anything."

"Sarah, come on."

"You lied to me, Bill. You lied about paying for the poetry. You lied about where the money came from. You lied about the mailbox. You lied about having a job with the city. You lied to me over and over and over."

"I lied, you're right. Let me tell you why. When I started going to the equipment shed, I came alive. I started writing again—writing with all my heart. The earthy smell, the clatter of metal tools, the guys on the crew—all that inspired me."

That's why he kept pretending he had a job. The shed became his studio away from his poetry-hating wife. That made a weird kind of sense to Ronald.

"I discovered I'm *bursting* with ideas—about love and death and God— the big stuff, Sarah. That's why I kept going back to the shed after they stopped paying me. I wrote with a confidence I haven't felt in years. Didn't you notice I was happier, more loving?"

"You mean you wanted to have sex?"

"Once again, you have misinterpreted what I said."

"I interpret you just fine, so listen to this. Get out of my house. Now!"

"You can't be serious. Right in front of a newspaper reporter? He's about to write a story about my new book." She stood immovable. Bill said to Ronald, "I'll call you at your office and you can ask me more questions about *Limbo*. Have you decided where the photo will be shot?"

Bill slammed the screen door. The Vega sputtered down the street.

"Never marry somebody who drives a piece of shit car. He can go to damn hell."

Damn hell—worse than regular hell. She kept talking. Ronald wasn't a reporter anymore since his resignation, but she didn't know that. He slid the notebook from his pants pocket.

CHAPTER THIRTY-THREE

On July 31st, Sarah was sleeping when a loud noise woke her up around two in the morning. She went to the front porch to see a fancy car on the edge of her yard, next to the fence. The birdbath was knocked down and deep tire tracks marked the lawn, which she'd just mown and raked.

"Bill slept through the whole thing," she said.

A man she'd never seen, dressed up and wearing a blazer and shiny loafers, staggered around her yard. When she asked if he was injured, he insulted her virtue, her hair, her home, and her flannel bathrobe. Then he offered to have sex with her, as if to show there were no hard feelings.

"He was drunk as a skunk." The hard-drinking forest animal would not go away.

A police car arrived and an officer spoke to the man. The man cursed the officer. Another police vehicle arrived and the man in the blazer got into it and was taken away. Within half an hour, a tow truck arrived and removed the wrecked car. Another officer drove up and put the broken pieces of the bird bath into a cardboard box. He was about to drive away, but Sarah objected, and he carried the box to her back porch, including the unbroken bowl.

"I called city hall the next day and told Ellen what happened," Sarah said.

"Ellen Swicegood, the police chief's secretary? You know her?"

"Ellen knows everybody. I told her, 'Somebody needs to put down some new turf in our front yard and buy us a new birdbath. We're talking about some big money.' Ellen said, 'You're right.' Next day, Lamont drove up in a different new car and knocked on the door."

In Sarah's mind, Ellen had ordered Lamont to do it. Maybe she had.

"Bill was home, of course, since he didn't have a job then, and we all went into the living room and sat down. Lamont was a total gentleman. He apologized for his words and said he was having a bad day, that he'd had a big argument with his son about something. He straight out asked me to forgive him. And I did because I'm a Christian and I believe in forgiveness."

Ronald could see it: Lamont doused with cologne, his rumbling baritone filling the room. In the threadbare house, he would have glowed like a celebrity.

"In a few minutes, it's like we were old friends. He asked how much it would cost to make the repairs and I told him a number. He pulled out his checkbook and wrote a check for that amount plus fifty dollars. He said, 'Is that enough?'"

Sarah smiled, relishing her seduction. Lamont did know how to get things done.

"We got around to talking about this and that. He asked Bill where he worked, and Bill said he was between jobs. Lamont said he might be able to get Bill a position with the city, if he was interested. Then Lamont said he had to run and asked Bill to walk to the car with him. They stood in the driveway laughing. They shook hands and Lamont drove away. Bill came back inside looking happy and said, 'I've got a job.'"

That was it, the description Ronald needed to write Lamontgate, straight from the eyewitness. His original story had come back to life. He jotted down her last two sentences, hoping he could read the scribbles when he sat down at the typewriter.

"Did Bill or Lamont say you shouldn't talk to the police about the wreck?" Ronald said.

"Lamont didn't say it, but we knew we shouldn't. We were just happy Bill had a job."

If a cop agency besides the Millerton police investigated, Bill and Sarah might get into legal trouble for taking what amounted to a bribe. Ronald didn't mention that.

"Sorry I ruined your anniversary dinner," he said.

"I guess I'll be calling a divorce lawyer soon. Do you know any?"

CHAPTER THIRTY-FOUR

Ronald chose his clothes with care the next day. Asking for his job back was kind of like a job interview. He settled on khaki pants and ditched his work boots for the hated penny loafers. But no tie. He wasn't that desperate. He applied hair cream to make his mane lie down, but he looked like a sellout. He took a second shower to wash it out. He smoked half a joint and walked into *The Eagle* newsroom at noon when he was sure Mr. Carlton and Martha would both be present. The room went quiet. Martha put down her coffee mug with a thump.

"Did you come back to clean out your desk?" she asked.

"I have returned to speak with you and Mr. Carlton."

Martha sighed and walked across the newsroom like Joan of Arc, her chin held high. Mr. Carlton watched them approach, his long face full of sorrow. Linda's phone rang. She lifted the receiver but dropped it back in the cradle so she could hear the conversation.

"I'm rescinding my resignation," Ronald said. He kept it short and sweet so he wouldn't babble. His bosses stared, their eyes like spotlights. Mr. Carlton's eyepatch gave him a gravitas Ronald had never felt before.

"Maybe you don't know it, Ronald, but this is a newspaper, not a motel you can check into and out of whenever you feel like it," Mr. Carlton said.

"I know that," Ronald replied. He wanted to say, "You mean like The Bates Motel in *Psycho,* where Janet Leigh gets stabbed in the shower? It's not that bad."

They stared some more, and Martha said, "Are you apologizing?"

"I made a mistake." Words for his tombstone.

Mr. Carlton looked away. It was Martha vs. Ronald.

"Are you saying you're sorry? If so, you're not doing a very good job of it," she said.

"I shouldn't have said those things I said. I regret my words." She kept drilling with her eyes. He couldn't get out of it. "I'm sorry."

Martha smirked, victorious. A win for her to savor.

"I guess I owe you an explanation for my behavior," Ronald said.

"You guess?" Martha said, pressing her advantage.

"When Danny showed me Bill Jorgensen's pay records, I was upset because my story fell apart. Then you spoke to me in a sharp tone. That hurts because I respect your opinion. But that's no excuse for my lack of professionalism. I crossed a line. Why did I do that? If you've got to know, my girlfriend and I had a big argument. We broke up. I was very upset. I'm not blaming you, Martha."

"Oh," Martha said, her tone softening. "I heard you were dating Monica Timbes, but I had no idea you two were that serious."

"We've talked about marriage." Meaning her marriage to Barry. "You know how being in a serious relationship can make you say and do crazy things."

That put Martha on the spot. She could say she understood, which would bring down the temperature, or say she didn't, which would be a tacit admission she'd never had a serious relationship. It would render her a romantic amateur. She said nothing.

"Why should we take you back?" Mr. Carlton demanded, returning to the conversation. "Give me one good reason."

"Two reasons. I regret my mistake. And I came across new information about Lamont that needs to get in the paper."

"You're never going to let that go, are you?"

"What's the new information?" Martha said.

"I had an on-the-record interview with Sarah Jorgensen. She says Lamont wrecked his car in her yard. He cursed her and a cop came by and took him home. The next day, Lamont came by their house and offered Bill the job with the city with the implicit understanding they'd keep quiet. That's what you said we needed to make the story happen. We have it."

"You interviewed her after you quit?" Mr. Carlton said. "Why?"

"Because I want to know the truth. I've worked too hard to let this story go down the drain. Millerton deserves to know. You, my editors, deserve to know."

He gave a full rundown of the interview, complete with Bill Jorgensen getting thrown out of the house.

"Did she say Lamont had been drinking?" Martha said.

"He was hammered as a hamster."

"A what?"

"She said he was drunk as a skunk, but I'm tired of that cliché."

"Don't make up quotes," Mr. Carlton said. "Martha and I will sit down and decide if we want to give you a second chance. Come back in an hour."

Mr. Carlton began typing. Martha returned to her desk and did the same. Ronald looked around the newsroom, now fond of the things that repelled him when he was first hired. The metal desks. They were army surplus, like you'd find on a military base. The beauty was that the newsroom was the opposite of a military base. You didn't have to call anybody sir. Nobody told you to keep your desk clean. Nobody complained when you thumbtacked a story with a dumb headline to the wall. The newsroom was a temple of free speech, except he couldn't tell dirty jokes when the women were around.

Snap, the perpetual dreamer, delivered a thumbs-up sign. Shelly pressed her hands together as if in prayer. Anne smiled a warm, motherly smile. Marcus pointed with one finger. Linda sat like a department store mannequin.

Ronald killed time reading magazines in the pharmacy. In *Cosmopolitan*, a French sexologist said anybody who didn't have simultaneous orgasms with their lover four times a week was doomed to mental illness. No wonder he felt so anxious. When he returned to the newsroom, Mr. Carlton and Martha were talking in low tones. Mr. Carlton waved him over.

"We're going to give you another chance," he said, not one to bury the lead. "You mishandled the Bill Jorgensen story, but we caught the problem in time. I hope you learned something from your mistake."

"I did." Check the documents first to avoid looking like an idiot.

"From now on, you've got to behave in a professional manner. We're starting your three-month probation period all over. You need to work closely with Martha and me. When you start your shift every morning, check with one of us to see if we have assignments. We're going to have you write about subjects that aren't on the police beat."

Ronald liked to come up with his own stories. Mr. Carlton's ideas were always about old stuff, history.

"When are we running the story about Lamont?" Ronald said.

"We're still not sure about the Lamont story. Until we're sure, we're putting it on the back burner."

"But I've got the eyewitness and the accident report. You said that's what we needed to publish. What else do you want?'

"We want to be sure," Mr. Carlton repeated.

Ronald spent a couple of hours writing and rewriting cop briefs, double-checking every address and date of birth. At the end of the day, he walked out of the office with Shelly as a massive sunset exploded behind city hall. She'd been curt since he declared war on poetry. Now she spoke.

"Man, you've got to get the Lamont story into print," she said in the parking lot. "That guy is impossible. Did you hear what happened at the last city council meeting? During the public comment section two people got up and complained because the council voted against repaving Millsaps Street. They said Lamont promised them he'd get the street repaved because it's full of potholes."

She dug into her handbag and pulled out a pack of Virginia Slims. Ronald shook out a Marlboro and lit both their cigarettes. They exhaled smoke skyward in unison.

"Lamont blamed it on me. He told the people my story mischaracterized him as being against the repaving. He called me out by name. So, I stood up and said, 'You voted against the project. You said it was too expensive,' which is true. And Lamont said he supports the project, just not right now while tax collections are low, and that my story didn't reflect the nuances of his position. And I said, 'I don't have to report everything you say. The story was accurate,' which it was. That idiot Stick said I was out of order and needed to sit down. I told Stick he should tell Lamont to stop lying. The big cop came over and laid his hand on my shoulder, like he was going to push me down into my chair."

"Joe Stoneman."

"Yeah. He's a gorilla. He's like eight feet taller than me. When the meeting was over, Lamont grabbed my arm and said I needed to write a follow-up story. I knocked his hand off and said, 'I'll decide what I'm writing, not you.' He said he'd call I.J. or Martha to complain, but he hasn't done it yet. If he touches me again, I'll knock his block off."

"Lamont's a jackass."

Ronald dropped his cigarette and ground it into the asphalt with his foot.

"Why did Mr. Carlton take me back if he doesn't want to run the Lamont story?" he said. "Getting that published is the one thing I want to do. This is such a wishy-washy way of doing things."

"Are you criticizing I.J. for being wishy-washy? He has trouble making decisions, just like you. I mean, Monica. I mean, the way you can't decide if Dwight is a good source or not."

"What am I supposed to do? Sit around and wait until Mr. Carlton changes his mind? I think I'm just going to quit the paper again."

"You can't give up, Ronald," Shelly said. "It's not just the story that's on the line. Your integrity, your soul, your very being is at stake. If you don't write this story, you might as well sell life insurance."

The insult jolted him. Selling life insurance was the opposite of being a journalist. Life insurance was based on fear and death, not hope and idealism. Ronald would do anything before he sold life insurance. Ditch digging. Prostitution. Public relations.

"You need to help I.J. make the decision," Shelly said.

Ronald went home and heated a can of chili on the stove. He smoked a joint in the bathroom. He drank two beers. He played records without the earphones. He looked at himself in the bathroom mirror for ten minutes. Then he picked up the phone.

CHAPTER THIRTY-FIVE

As predicted, Mr. Carlton gave Ronald a story assignment the next day. He was supposed to profile a Methodist minister's widow who had collected every copy of *The Upper Room,* the church's devotional magazine.

"This will help expand your reporting skills," Mr. Carlton said.

"I'm agnostic. I'm incapable of writing the story."

Mr. Carlton wouldn't budge. Ronald was dialing to set up the interview when Mr. Carlton told him to put down the phone.

"There's a TV van parked outside city hall," he said. "Martha, call Dot Smith and find out what's going on. Ronald, trot over to the police station and ask around."

Ronald looked out the window. "It's Channel 5."

"Damn. Get moving."

Betty Stokes rose as soon as Ronald stepped up to the front desk. She handed him the clipboard and he started flipping through reports.

"One of my sources told me Miss Dawn Mourning from Channel 5 is interviewing Chief Jim Smithers right now," she said.

Betty grinned. A tiny bit of the feminine, Mantovani-loving Betty peeked out from beneath her neutered cop exterior. Her everything-in-life-is-personal philosophy felt morally wrong, but he'd learned something from her. You had to be sneaky to survive in the adult world. Honest maybe, but never naive.

"What are Dawn and the chief talking about?"

"I don't know. She just got here. It could be about an automobile accident involving an unidentified member of the city council."

"I wonder who tipped Channel 5."

Betty said it wasn't her. Ronald walked across the parking lot separating city hall and *The Eagle*. All eyes turned toward him when he opened the newsroom door. Mr. Carlton put down his pipe, and Martha stood up at her desk.

"Dawn Mourning is in Chief Smithers's office," he said.

"Damn," Mr. Carlton said. He stared out the window again. If Channel 5 scooped *The Eagle* one more time it would be a hari-kari moment for I.J. Carlton. Everybody in the newsroom knew that one of his core beliefs—stronger than Jesus being his lord and savior—was that television news people didn't know what they were doing. To find their stories, they just picked up the newspaper. If TV broke a story *The Eagle* didn't have, his world would be turned upside down. Gravity would cease to exist, and his pipes would lift to the ceiling.

"We need to find out what this is about," Mr. Carlton said. "The clock is working against us. If she finds something big and reports it at eleven o'clock, well, she's beat us fair and square. There's nothing we can do about it. But if she reports it at six o'clock, we'll have time to match it in tomorrow's paper. Then we won't look like we're out of touch with what's happening in our own backyard. We sure as hell can't wait until the day after. That would make us look like a bunch of clowns."

"How can we watch her story?" Ronald asked. "We don't have a TV in the office."

"I'll call my wife and ask her to watch Channel 5 the rest of the day."

"Betty Stokes thinks it may be about Lamont's wreck," Ronald said.

"I bet you're right. If they break that story and everybody knows we've been sitting on it, we'll look bad. How much have you written?"

Ronald didn't have a decent lead. "Almost finished," he said.

"Good. Have you ever met Dawn Mourning?"

"Once, briefly, after the Joe Butler fiasco. She's good-looking, but a lightweight as a reporter."

"She's a total babe," Snap called out. "Really built."

"Go over to city hall and strike up a conversation with her. Find out what she's working on," Mr. Carlton said.

Ronald scampered back to the police station. Betty was standing at the counter.

"Is she still with the chief?" he said.

"She went to the city manager's office."

Ronald didn't want to go there. He figured Danny was still sore about him and Stick going into Danny's private office a few days ago. He didn't want to get yelled at, not in front of Dawn Mourning. He sat down on the front steps of city hall and waited until she came out fifteen minutes later.

"Well, hello there," she said, as if bumping into Ronald had made her day. She glowed in her bottle blondeness, but this time she wore a forest green blazer and had turned down the volume on her lipstick.

Ronald stood. "Hi, Dawn. Great to see you again. What brings you to our fair city?"

"Man, it's so hot standing here. Could we go somewhere and get a Coke?"

They settled into a window booth at the Millerton Diner while her camera guy sat in the van. The cooks came out of the kitchen to grab a look at the TV woman.

"What are you working on?" she said.

"A story about a Methodist minister's widow who owns every copy of *The Upper Room* ever printed. It's the Methodist devotional. Have you read it?"

"I was raised Catholic in Indiana, so no, I haven't."

"It's kind of a dumb story, but on a paper like *The Eagle* you have to write some little league stuff now and then."

"I'll look for your story. I read *The Eagle* all the time. You're good. You're the best reporter on the paper. You're a real writer. Your police briefs are like short stories—like Chekhov in miniature."

Supercharged flattery, meaning she got nothing out of Danny or Chief Smithers.

"Thanks. I liked your story about the patient who strangled her rheumatologist in Winston-Salem," Ronald said. "What are you working on now?"

"I'm chasing a tip about a city government scandal," she said and twirled her hair with one finger. "Somebody called in an anonymous tip to the station. The news director sent me out here since I've gotten some scoops in Millerton before. But the city manager and the police chief don't know anything or say they don't." She sipped Coke through a straw. "It involves a member of the city council, but I don't know which one. Are any of them kind of shady?"

Her sky-blue eyes were mesmerizing. The safety catches on his brain began disengaging. He wanted to impress her, to win her favor, but his self-preservation instincts kicked in at the last minute. It was his story.

"I don't cover the city council," he said.

She looked at him with a steady gaze. "Here's something you will know. I'm looking for an ex-cop named Dwight Bennett. Since you're the police reporter, you must know where I could find him."

Who told her about Dwight? When Ronald called in the anonymous tip to Channel 5, he didn't mention Dwight's name. That meant she had a source of her own somewhere in Millerton.

"I've heard of Dwight," he said, fashioning a non-denial denial on the spot. "He's a jerk, and some people say he's a liar. The chief said he canned Dwight for doing dishonest things."

"I'd still like to talk with him, so if you come across his phone number somewhere, let me know." She slid a business card across the table. "And give me a call if you're interested in working for Channel 5. The station is always looking for good newswriters. I'll pave the way with the news director. TV is the future of news."

He slipped the card into his shirt pocket. Maybe she had figured out he was the anonymous tipster and this was her way of repaying him.

"Thanks, Dawn, but I'm a print man."

"Ink in your veins, huh? I can respect that."

She let him pay for the Cokes. In the parking lot, Dawn shook his hand and got into the van.

Again, Ronald was the center of attention when he returned to the newsroom. He described the conversation with Dawn.

"We may need to run the story tomorrow," Mr. Carlton said. He walked a circuit around the office. He wasn't ready to commit yet. "But she doesn't know it's Lamont, does she?"

"Not yet. But the wreck is an open secret in Millerton. It won't be hard to find somebody who'll tell her."

"That's true." Mr. Carlton paused to pick up one of Shelly's snow globes. She had a collection of eight arranged on a small shelving unit on her desk.

"Dawn's looking for Dwight," Ronald said. "She asked me how to find him. I'm trying to figure out who tipped her. It could be a thousand people."

"Wow. She knows the name of our source. Did you tell her how to find him?"

"Of course not, but if she does find him—and it wouldn't be hard to do—there's no telling what he'll say. Dwight's been threatening to take the story to TV."

Mr. Carlton clapped his hands once.

"That decides it. We're running Lamont tomorrow," he said. "It's the lead story, with a headline stripped across the top. We'll run a one-column mugshot of Lamont. We'll hold the story about new fire extinguishers at the elementary school to make room. Ronald, finish your story."

CHAPTER
THIRTY-SIX

Snap announced he was buying as soon as they stepped into Exiles. Ronald spread a front page proof on the table to admire his work. Shelly sat down beside him and read the headline aloud: "Councilman Moody Wrecked Car But Not Prosecuted." She sang the lead, "Millerton City Councilman Lamont Moody wasn't investigated for driving under the influence when he wrecked his personal automobile in an Archdale Street yard, though the resident said Moody was drinking alcohol that night and acted"—she took a breath and shouted—"'drunk as a skunk.'"

Everybody in the bar whooped. Ronald had read the lead to himself a dozen times in the office, but hearing the words spoken aloud by somebody else made them powerful and beautiful, like literature. Maybe Dawn's assessment of his writing wasn't just flattery. When the paper was printed tomorrow, he'd grab twenty copies to send out with résumés. He'd quit *The Eagle* within a month.

"You're Millerton's version of Carl Bernstein and Bill Woodward," she said.

"*Bob* Woodward," Ronald said.

"Okay, Bob Woodward. If you say so."

Marcus took a picture of Ronald, Snap, and Shelly toasting, using the little Nikon he carried everywhere, then Snap took a photo with Marcus in the picture. Snap bought more beer. Ronald bought beer. Marcus bought beer. A foosball challenge was issued, and Marcus knocked the ball off the table with a power shot. Snap stuck the ball into his belly button, then used an abdominal thrust to shoot it back onto the table. Snap plugged money into the jukebox and played air guitar. Shelly danced by herself. Marcus screeched, "Free Bird!"—perhaps the first time in history a Black man had uttered those words in a beer joint. They sat down, winded.

"I saw something weird on the way over," Snap said. "Dwight was driving down the street in his Cutlass and there was a woman sitting in the car next to him. And you know who it looked like? Linda."

"Our Linda?" Ronald said. "Get real. She has a crush on Dwight from long ago, but she's not his type."

"Linda and Dwight," Shelly said, exhaling one last puff of smoke, "are dating. It's official."

Ronald had no idea. Would this mess up his story? Was Linda telling Dwight stuff behind Ronald's back? Shelly went to the ladies' room. Ronald waited outside the bathroom door for her to come out.

"Why didn't you tell me Linda and Dwight were dating?" he said. "That feels like a major conflict of interest."

"Don't worry. It's helping you. Dwight was furious with you for talking to Chief Smithers."

"I know. He called me to cuss me out."

"Another police department is talking to him about a job. He worried the story would mess up his chances of getting hired, but Linda told him to cool down and he did."

Ronald absorbed the information and said, "Do you think she's dating Dwight to help me?"

Shelly laughed and took Ronald's hands in her damp fingers.

"No. Linda's carried a torch for Dwight for years—don't ask me why. You're benefiting, but it's coincidental that your journalistic ambitions and her sexual aims are in alignment. Sit back and let it happen. For once you got a break."

Ronald felt uneasy. Unseen forces were controlling his life.

CHAPTER
THIRTY-SEVEN

Snap said they should go to The Food Mart. Shelly and Marcus climbed into Ronald's car and they took side streets so they could smoke a joint on the way. Ronald was anxious. He'd never seen a Black person or a woman drinking beer behind The Food Mart. They bought 16-ounce Budweisers and walked through the backdoor to find half a dozen regulars standing there with beer cans in their hands. The men looked at the people who didn't fit in. Shelly and Marcus.

"What is this?" Shelly said. "It looks like a parking lot."

"It's an outdoor bar," Ronald said. "It's cool."

"It smells like a bathroom."

"That's because guys piss against the dumpster."

"Introduce me to your friends," she said.

A guy called Marcus's name and they shook like they knew each other. A football joke was told. Everybody went back to talking and drinking. Harold Jameson, the well-dressed businessman who first advised Ronald to contact Dwight Bennett, walked over with Reggie, who was wearing his hunting cap, as always.

"I heard you got Lamont!" Jameson said and shook Ronald's hand. "Brilliant reporting. Top-flight journalism."

"How'd you know? The paper hasn't come off the presses yet."

"Anne, your women's editor, is friends with my old lady. Didn't you know that?"

Ronald didn't. Millerton was smaller than he realized, and his blind spots were bigger.

"What do you think he'll be indicted on?" Jameson said. "Bribery? Leaving the scene of an accident? I hope he goes to prison for the rest of his life."

"Come on, man," Reggie said to Jameson. "Go easy on Lamont. He had a wreck and the cops gave him a ride home. Is that so bad? I'm sure you drove around drunk and got a free pass when you were on the city council."

"Just once or twice," Jameson said, shrugging.

"Are you telling me," Ronald said to Jameson, "that you drove drunk and the cops covered it up? You've been acting like Lamont was public enemy number one because he did that."

"But I didn't get caught, man, that's all that matters. You've just got to know the right people, and I do."

The face slap of cynicism froze Ronald in his spot. Back when Jameson suggested Ronald contact Dwight, it was an act of political opportunism. Ronald had been a pawn, not a white knight.

"Don't be mad," Jameson said. "This will work out for you. When Lamont steps down, I'll run for his council seat. You'll have a direct pipeline into what happens on the city council. You'll get scoop after scoop. I promise."

"Your worldview is perverse," Ronald said. "Don't you understand that ..."

The squeal of tires split the air, followed by the metal-on-metal clamor of motor vehicles colliding. Without a word, the beer-drinkers rushed into the store and out the front door.

"Where's everybody going?" Shelly asked, but she followed.

Ronald had visited dozens of wreck scenes, yet he'd never seen one seconds after it happened while the engines hissed and the headlight glass tinkled. He started writing the cop brief in his head. The driver of the green car had crossed the center line and powered into the left front headlight of an oncoming yellow Rambler Ambassador station wagon, a sturdy kidmobile with fake wood built into the sides.

"Damn," Marcus yelled and ran toward the station wagon. "Miss Rosie!"

He yanked open the driver's door and a woman wearing a white nurse's uniform with thick-soled shoes stepped out. It was Rosie Mitchell, the supervising nurse at the hospital emergency room. Ronald phoned her almost every day to get the medical condition of people hurt in wrecks. She began addressing grievances at the green car, the guys standing in front of The Food Mart, and the world at large. Ronald gathered she'd just finished paying off the station wagon.

"Is she okay?" Shelly called out. "Do we need to call an ambulance?"

"I don't think so," Marcus said. "She was the nurse when I broke my ankle in high school playing football. She and my mother are friends."

The driver's door creaked open on the green car, a Bonneville coupe. Lamont Moody put both feet on the ground, grasped the door frame with one hand and pulled himself to a standing position. He put a can of Pabst Blue Ribbon beer on the car roof, positioned both hands on his hips, and arched his back, sighing with relief.

"Where's your camera?" Ronald said to Marcus.

"In your car, under the seat," Marcus said. "I didn't bring it into this place because I ..."

Ronald handed him the key. "Get it."

Lamont stretched his neck, looking right at home. He wore a houndstooth sport coat, charcoal slacks, and alligator loafers, like he'd just closed a deal.

"Look at this," Jameson yelled from the front of The Food Mart, gesturing with his own beer can. "Lamont Moody, three sheets to the wind."

"You're one to talk," Lamont yelled back. Spotting Ronald and Shelly, he said, "And the whole newspaper staff is here getting drunk too. Isn't this cozy? What other lies are you telling about me, you lying hippie?"

"Who are you calling a liar?" Shelly said.

"I'm calling you one. You're a lying hippie bitch. Everything you write in The Eaglet is a lie. And everything Ronald Truluck writes is a lie."

Sirens sang in the distance. With the wreck blocking the two-lane road, drivers got out of their cars to see what had happened. Shelly walked up to Lamont and stood in front of him. The crowd's decibel level dropped.

"Excuse me," she said. "Did you just call me a bitch?"

Her voice was calm and cool. Everybody heard her question to Lamont. Shelly stood firm in her turtleneck-jeans uniform. Lamont was a foot taller, with a sagging beer gut and drooping mustache. Ronald was torn. Step up to protect his female best friend or remain a detached observer?

"What about it?" Lamont said. "It's the truth. Why don't you calm yourself down?"

"Why don't you learn to respect women, you son of a bitch?" Shelly said.

Lamont's smile disappeared. He slipped off his sport coat and tossed it onto his open car door.

"Oh God, he's going to hit her," somebody whispered.

"Don't talk about my mother that way," Lamont said, reverting to school-boy repartee.

"I feel sorry for your mother for having you," Shelly shot back.

Lamont lurched forward with his chest thrust out, as if to intimidate Shelly. Ronald didn't see what was coming next. Neither did Lamont. Shelly planted her right foot on the asphalt and used her forward momentum to propel her right fist straight into Lamont's nose. The smack of flesh on flesh coincided with the click of Marcus's camera.

"Whoa!" The Food Mart chorus said.

Lamont stumbled backward and landed on his butt. He rolled onto his side, groaning and holding his hands to his face.

"Good one, Shelly," Marcus shouted and moved in to shoot more pictures.

Shelly stood over Lamont and yelled, "How do you like getting your ass kicked by a woman? Get used to it, motherfucker. This is the future!"

She shook her finger. Motorists honked their horns. The scene was spinning into chaos.

"Cool it, Shelly. You're showing animus," Ronald said, remembering a word from a journalism class on libel law. "If you say negative things about the subject of a news story, it can come back to bite you in court if the subject of the news story files a lawsuit. Be neutral."

"Screw neutral!" she screamed.

Lamont sat up, steadying himself with one palm on the pavement. His words were indecipherable. Ronald intuited Lamont was saying he would gain revenge one day.

"Lamont sucks," Shelly yelled to Ronald. "You told me so. You called him a cretin and a sleaze and a dirtbag and a drunk and said he cheated on his wife."

Lamont looked at Ronald like he was a friend who'd betrayed him.

"Sorry, Lamont," Ronald said. "You do drink a lot."

Jameson grabbed Ronald's arm. "Drink a lot?" he said. "Lamont's the drunkest bastard in all of Miller County. In all of North Carolina. In all of ..."

The first Millerton cop arrived with a whooping siren. Joe Stoneman swept his eyes over the growing crowd of spectators and went straight to Lamont.

"That woman sucker punched me," Lamont told him. Stoneman hooked his arms under Lamont's armpits and lifted him to his feet.

"He's too drunk to be hurt," Shelly said. "Throw him in jail."

"Shut up, lady," Stoneman yelled. "Move away and wait for me to take your statement. Remember, you're a suspect in a criminal matter."

Shelly retreated to the far side of the two-lane road and rubbed her punching hand. Stoneman turned back to Lamont, who'd gone into his Bonneville and retrieved a pack of cigarettes. The beer can Ronald earlier saw on the car roof had disappeared.

Another patrol car arrived. Andy Anderson, a young cop Ronald knew, and Clete Crenshaw, the only Black cop in Millerton, ordered the crowd of spectators to move back, though nobody was trying to move forward. With the wreck blocking traffic, more drivers stopped and got out of their cars to view the scene. The crowd had doubled in size.

Marcus lay low. Clete filled out the accident report on a clipboard while Stoneman stood over his shoulder giving instruction.

"Will Lamont be charged with drunk driving?" Ronald asked Andy.

"Doubt it. Stoneman will say Lamont didn't look drunk so there's no probable cause."

"Everybody saw him drinking."

Andy winked. "Judgment call."

An unspoken conspiracy was happening right before Ronald's eyes. Everybody knew their part without being told. But Ronald knew something Andy didn't. Marcus had taken pictures.

A tow truck arrived and lifted the Bonneville. Lamont beamed his salesman grin at Stoneman. Ronald walked up to Lamont and said, "How much have you had to drink tonight?"

"Who says I was drinking?" Lamont said.

"You got out of your car with a beer can in your hand. I saw it."

"That doesn't mean I was drinking beer. Sometimes I find an empty can on the side of the road and pick it up because I hate to see litter. What's wrong with that?" Lamont contained more bullshit than Saudi Arabia had oil.

"You made a left turn into an oncoming car. Were you going to The Food Mart to drink more beer?"

"None of your business where I was going. This is a free country and if you don't like it, you can move back to Russia—or Chapel Hill."

Jameson strode up, shaking his finger at Lamont.

"I just took a peek inside your car and I saw three Blue Ribbon cans and a half-empty pint of Jim Beam."

"You planted those cans, you lowdown polecat."

"You're done for, Lamont. You'll be thrown off the city council. Your wife will divorce you. Your children won't speak to you. Your business will go down the toilet. You'll be sleeping under a bridge."

"Face facts," Lamont said to Jameson. "I'm a better councilman than you were. In fact, I'm a better *man* than you in every single way. Just ask your wife."

Though Jameson was drunk, his right jab was as quick and efficient as an engine piston. Lamont staggered backward and sat down on the pavement a second time. As the crowd encircled the men, Lamont kicked at

Jameson so hard his loafer flew off. Seeing a street fight between two middle-aged men in business clothes was a first for Ronald.

Stoneman sprinted and smacked into Jameson with a flying tackle—a football player reverting to training. The impact carried them onto the asphalt and, after three seconds of grunting, Stoneman exerted his size advantage. Stoneman pulled Jameson's arms into handcuffing position. Marcus reappeared and shot pictures, moving in a radius around the wiggling bodies. Clete Crenshaw helped control Jameson. Andy, the young cop, saw Marcus taking pictures and said, "Hey, stop that. No pictures!" Marcus backed away. Andy advanced on Marcus with his hand out. "Give me the camera," he commanded. Marcus turned and ran. Andy ran after him.

Ronald didn't have time to think about neutrality. He tackled Andy from behind and wrapped his arms around his midsection. He lost his balance and pulled Andy down to the asphalt with him. Marcus disappeared into the shadows.

"Dammit," Andy said and punched Ronald in the face. He prepared to punch again but Stoneman yelled he needed help controlling Jameson. Ronald stood and rubbed his cheek. He hadn't been punched since the eighth grade.

The cops lifted Jameson to a standing position, his hands cuffed behind his back. His shirt was ripped, and his black hair fell into his eyes. He unfurled a litany of curses about the minuscule size of police penises. A black unmarked car pulled up. Sheriff Hawk Hawkins and his chief deputy, Sammy Nichols, emerged. It was now a multi-departmental crime scene, meaning there would be more than one version of what happened. The assembled cops parted for Hawk as he took a position in front of Jameson.

"What the hell did you do, Jameson?" Hawk said.

"I got into a tussle with Lamont and these gorillas took his side and tackled me. It's police brutality, Hawk. This should not happen."

"What happened, Mr. Eagle?"

"I heard a collision and came out to make sure nobody was hurt. Lamont Moody and Shelly, my colleague, got into an argument," Ronald said. "It got physical."

"Are you saying Lamont hit this Shelly woman?"

"He tried to," Shelly said. "I smacked him right in the snoot."

"You punched Lamont?" Hawk said, his face revealing his glee.

"She sucker punched me," Lamont cried out. "You know I can whip half the men in this county and all the women."

Hawk shook his head. "Not all of them."

CHAPTER THIRTY-EIGHT

Ronald started early the next day so he could write a reaction story about his story about Lamont's wreck. He found none of the outrage he expected. Wendell Burgess, an electrical contractor, summed up the public mood.

"He didn't kill nobody," Wendell said between forkfuls of scrambled eggs at the diner. "Lamont just ran off the road. Everybody's done that at some time in their lives."

"But the police gave him special treatment," Ronald said. "They put him above the law. You don't want that, do you?"

"The way I see it, people serving on the council are already giving a lot of their time to the city and so they've earned a break from the police now and then. God knows I couldn't stand to sit through those meetings. If it was something big, like killing somebody, I'd feel different. But for a wreck like that, I don't have a problem with the police not writing up Lamont."

No wonder the cops felt so comfortable covering up for Lamont. That's what the public expected. But Lamontgate didn't matter. It had been upstaged by the wildfire rumors about The Food Mart punch out, though that story and picture wouldn't run until the next day. Police corruption was nothing compared to Shelly's mighty fist. When a male public official was knocked down by an angry woman, the public was inflamed—or at least titillated. It was news.

"If I was Lamont, I'd be ashamed to show my face in public ever again," Wendell said. "A man just can't let that kind of thing happen to him. It destroys confidence in the government and in society. Next time I see Lamont, I'll tell him that."

Nobody at *The Eagle* cared about anything else.

"What I heard," Martha said, pacing in front of Ronald's desk, "is Lamont smashed a longneck beer bottle on the hood of his car and said, 'I'm going to kill you, woman.' But Shelly kicked him in the, well, the groin area of his body, and Lamont fell and lay on the street crying like a baby until the police came and took him to the hospital. Now he's talking about filing a lawsuit against her."

"Will he be able to father children again?" asked Anne, the women's editor. "Because a friend told me that kind of injury can cause permanent damage."

Ronald was happy people were obsessed with the punchout instead of Lamontgate. Errors had slipped into his story in the deadline rush. The second paragraph said the wreck at Bill Jorgensen's house occurred on July 32nd. A photo caption referred to Lamont Moody as Lamont Noomy. Worst of all, Ronald forgot he'd promised to keep Dwight Bennett anonymous. He named him four times in print. Ronald called to apologize.

"I'm sorry," Ronald said. "I promised to keep your identity secret and I failed. I've brought shame upon myself, *The Eagle*, and the entire profession of journalism."

"How did it happen?"

"I was in a hurry. Deadline pressure. But that's no excuse. This will keep me awake at night for the rest of my life. I feel a crippling guilt over the problems this may cause for you. If it prevents you from getting another police job, I'll never forgive myself."

"Don't worry about it. Everything is fine."

"Is this the Dwight Bennett who stood on his balcony and yelled at me? Who said I promised to keep his name out of the story and I had better keep my promise?"

"It's me. Your story makes me look pretty good. Like I was an honest officer just doing my job. The main thing is the story didn't stop me from getting another job. Anyway, tell me about Shelly knocking down Lamont. I would have given a million dollars to see that happen."

Once again, Ronald sensed unknown forces were controlling his life. Something was happening, but he didn't know what.

Marcus walked in with pictures in hand. He ignored Ronald, the expert on all things Lamont, and laid the photos on Mr. Carlton's desk. Everybody got up to look. The story had turned into a group project.

"These are nice pictures," Mr. Carlton said. He rarely exuded such emotion. Everyone murmured in agreement except Shelly.

"We're glorifying violence if we run these pictures in the paper," Shelly said with a wave of her bruised, wrapped hand. "They're awful. What will people say about me? They'll think I'm some kind of thug. I've never punched anybody in my life."

"These pictures fit my story. And you look great in the picture," Ronald said. If anybody else was going to get credit for taking down Lamont, Ronald wanted it to be Shelly.

She went back to her desk, pretending to sulk. In reality, she was thrilled to be the center of attention and a heroine. Several women had called to compliment her for standing up to a male chauvinist. Nobody criticized her for being violent.

"Which one's the lead picture?" Ronald asked, picking up the print of Shelly's punch. It was a magnificent photo, but Ronald couldn't say so. If he did, Marcus's ego would inflate to Hindenburg proportions and crush all of them against the newsroom walls.

"Marcus, what do you think?" Mr. Carlton said.

"The one of Shelly slugging Lamont. That one required perfect timing, perfect positioning." Marcus took the print from Ronald's hands and held it close to his face. "You don't see a picture like this every day. Have you ever seen the photo of the man in the hat shooting the guy who shot President Kennedy?"

"You mean Jack Ruby killing Lee Harvey Oswald, one of the most famous news photographs of all time?" Ronald said.

"My picture is just like that. It's a split second frozen in time."

"Martha and I will decide which pictures to use," Mr. Carlton said. "Now get back to work, both of you. How soon will you have the copy, Ronald?"

#

The double doors to the police department creaked open and he stepped into the familiar lobby stench. Betty stood and hitched up her police pants like a cowboy. She handed him the clipboard.

"Good work," she said. "Lamont's a goner."

Ronald blushed. Betty was the first person to compliment his investigation since the paper was published.

"I need to get the accident report from the wreck that happened last night at The Food Mart," he said.

"Maybe you should just go to the press conference at two o'clock in the city council chambers. Everybody's going to be there. Chief Smithers, Mayor Stick, Sheriff Hawk, the district attorney, President Ford, and Donald Duck."

"Nobody told me. Are they trying to keep me out? That's illegal. I'll call the newspaper lawyer myself and ..."

"The chief didn't decide until thirty minutes ago. Ellen Swicegood may be calling your office right now, acting like she and I.J. Carlton are best friends. She can be sweet as pie when it serves her purpose."

A whole press conference called because of Ronald. When he stepped into the newsroom, Martha whipped her head around, eyes shining.

"I know, two o'clock in council chambers," Ronald said, depriving her of one of the sweetest rewards of journalism: telling another journalist something they should already know.

"Do you know what will happen at the press conference? Because I do," Martha said, preening.

"How could you possibly know?"

"Danny told Dot and Dot told me."

She returned to her desk. Ronald followed.

"Would you mind telling me what will happen?"

She turned to face Ronald. "Chief Smithers is going to announce that Lamont will be charged with reckless driving and public drinking for running into Rosie's car last night. They'll charge him with reckless driving and property damage for wrecking in the Jorgensen's yard on July 31st. The district attorney will say he's going to fast track the cases because public officials should not receive preferential treatment. Stick will demand Lamont step down from the city council while the cases go through the court system. If he doesn't, Stick will take action to have him suspended."

"That's a lot."

"And the city will present Shelly with bronzed boxing gloves."

"How'd they get those made so fast?"

Martha, suddenly a deadpan artist, went back to typing.

The press conference went down as she predicted. Reporters from two TV stations as well as the Winston-Salem and Greensboro papers showed up. All Ronald had to do was fill in the blanks with quotes about integrity, public trust, and no person being above the law. Nobody talked about Lamont being outdone by a woman, but Chief Smithers got a laugh when he said Lamont "tried to skirt the law."

Ellen Swicegood, the champion of public records, distributed the accident report on Lamont's wreck in the Jorgensen's front yard—the report Ronald got through hours of investigative reporting. But this one was certified by the chief, ensuring nobody would bother to mention Ronald's version. Ellen beamed at Ronald, whispering into his ear, "You brought a bad guy to justice! Thanks to you, Millerton is a better place to live."

Stick advanced to the podium and said, "Chief Smithers has told me things about Lamont Moody that are simply dramastic. Lamont needs to step down from the city council, or I'll get him impeached."

Dawn Mourning stood. "Were the things you heard dramatic or fantastic?"

"Both."

"Does Millerton have an impeachment process?" she asked.

"If we don't, we'll get one. Danny, do we have an impeachment process?"

"At this time, the city doesn't have an impeachment process similar to the impeachment process employed by the federal government," Danny said.

"We need an impeachment process by tomorrow," Stick said.

"If Lamont resigns, we won't have to impeach him, Mayor. Why don't we wait?"

"If you can't make it happen, maybe we need a new city manager."

Arthur Fleetwood Sr., the city attorney, said, "Let me look into the legalities first, Mayor."

"Thank you, Arthur. Good to know I can depend on somebody." Stick sat down.

Without prompting, the men in suits gathered for handshake photos. Sheriff Hawk delivered a thumbs-up as he walked out.

CHAPTER THIRTY-NINE

"Moody Knocked Out of Office" roared the wall-to-wall headline in the next day's paper, since a news event of this magnitude demanded a pun. Ronald's lead said, "Lamont Moody resigned his position on the Millerton City Council in disgrace and will be charged in two auto accidents, it was announced at a city hall press conference attended by a multitude of city and county officials. These thunderbolt developments occurred after Moody had the second wreck—a two-car collision in front of The Food Mart—and was struck in the face by an employee of *The Eagle*. Moments earlier, Moody had insulted the employee with disrespectful words that cannot be printed in a family newspaper. Moody was treated at the scene and not hospitalized."

Ronald insisted on using "in disgrace" because it was found in almost every breaking news story about Nixon's resignation. Mr. Carlton put up a little resistance, then yielded.

The words were inconsequential. Marcus's stark black-and-white picture told the story. It captured the droopy flesh of Lamont's face conforming to Shelly's knuckles like an old boxing photo. Her lips were pulled back in a snarl while her peace sign pendant bounced on its chain. In the background, drinkers from The Food Mart, including Ronald and Snap, watched open-mouthed.

Martha had wanted to run the picture a gargantuan five columns, a size last used when a Millerton girl won the Miss North Carolina pageant, but Mr. Carlton made her take it down to four columns. "No need to rub it in," he said. "He's been humiliated enough."

Before he left the office, Ronald mustered the energy to argue with his editors about the next step. Ronald wanted to get Chief Smithers fired for overseeing an ongoing pattern of corruption in the police department—and for switching the names on the Joe Butler accident report.

"Hold your horses," Mr. Carlton said. "In the end, the chief did the right thing, so let's not punish him. He's got a hard job being police chief. Another thing, people have a limited appetite for hearing about corruption. When they pick up *The Eagle*, they want to hear about lost cats being found and someone's granddaughter getting a perfect attendance medal at school and stuff like that. If they want to hear about government corruption day after day, they can subscribe to *The Washington Post*. And by the way, how are you doing with the feature about the widow with all the copies of *The Upper Room*?"

He packed his pipe, then sat back and puffed. Ronald had never heard the editor deliver a soliloquy of this length. It was a statement of his beliefs. Do the right thing, but don't go overboard. Whether Ronald liked it or not, this story was the high mark of his time at *The Eagle*. When his shift ended, he grabbed twenty copies of that day's paper to send out with résumés.

He drove to Monica's house. She opened the front door and said, "We don't want any," like he was a teenager selling magazine subscriptions for band camp. She shone in a white Beatles T-shirt. He held up a copy of the paper.

"I got my job back. I wrote the story. Lamont Moody is quitting the city council. I was passing by your place and decided to stop and say thanks for the tip."

"My shitty tip?" Monica said and recited verbatim their previous front porch conversation. Maybe she'd tape-recorded his words.

"If I said 'shitty,' I shouldn't have," Ronald said. "Sorry."

"There's no 'if.' You said it." Her stare burned like a high-intensity flashlight. It differed from a cop stare or a boss stare because the implied threat was psychological destruction, not arrest or firing. "If the tip was so bad, how did you achieve such resounding professional success?"

"It's a complicated explanation. Could we talk about it?"

They drove into the country at dusk, the transition period when Ronald felt most comfortable. Monica sat far away on the bench seat with her hands clasped in her lap. Ronald described the sequence of events.

"Your tip had everything to do with the way things worked out. All things are connected, right? Your tip triggered the chain of events. It wasn't an accurate tip, but you meant to give me a good tip and lo and behold, a good thing happened. Life is a series of unintended consequences. All we can do is start out the right way. Intention is everything. So, thank you."

"You're welcome, I guess," she said and sounded calmer.

"And I forgive you for the cruel things you said to me. You don't have to apologize."

"Why should I apologize to you? Okay, I didn't tell you I'm married, but so what? You don't care if I'm married or not. What you're doing is a pitiful attempt at getting out of giving me a heartfelt apology. You're an amateur at this. You've never broken up with a girl and then made up with her, have you?"

"Of course I have." In college he'd gone on a blind date with a girl who talked nonstop about the boyfriend who'd just dumped her and then started making fun of Ronald's sideburns, so he excused himself to go to the bathroom and walked out the back door of the pizza joint. They passed on campus the next two semesters and always nodded to each other in a friendly manner. "Besides, what have I got to apologize for?"

"For dumping me with no warning when I did nothing wrong," Monica said. "For saying hurtful things. For blaming me for the tip, which by your own admission worked out just fine."

Monica had a deep bag of breakup tricks. She was using his own bullshit against him.

"Would you apologize for saying you hope I wreck my car in a lake and drown?" he said.

"A river. I said I hoped you wreck your car in a river. It was obvious hyperbole spoken in a moment of high emotion. How could you take such a comment seriously?"

High emotion. An admission she cared.

"Because there was an implication of violence," he said. "And you said I don't know as much as you do about books like *The Great Gatsby*. That's true, but you went overboard with it. You talk like you're the professor and I'm a freshman. Will you apologize for having a condescending attitude?"

"Never." She said it with unwavering conviction, like he'd asked her to betray her country for a pittance.

That did it. He couldn't stand her intellectual arrogance any longer. They'd spent hours talking about books and movies, mostly while driving through the country, but she rarely listened to what he had to say. He was going to end it. Before he could say another word, the patrol car lights flashed in his rearview mirror.

CHAPTER FORTY

Ronald pulled his car into the parking lot of an abandoned country store. No houses in sight. He readied his license and registration.

"What's going on?" Monica said. "How fast were you going?"

They had left Millerton behind and entered the vast, dark territory of the county. They were outside the jurisdiction of the Millerton police. That meant the cop was either a sheriff's deputy or a state patrolman. Ronald hadn't been drinking or smoking dope. He wasn't carrying any drugs.

"Eagle, I told you to mind your own business," Joe Stoneman said when he reached the side of the Galaxie. "Look at all the trouble you've made."

"Ronald, what is he saying?" Monica whispered. "Are we going to get arrested?"

"What are you doing here, Joe? We're in the county," Ronald said, knowing how weak that protest sounded. Jurisdiction counted for nothing when revenge was involved. In the rearview mirror he caught a flash of light as the passenger door opened on the patrol car. A chunky body stepped out. Turkey Stoneman, Lamont's muscle, sauntered up beside his brother.

"Get out of the car—both of you," Joe said.

Ronald complied and shut the driver's door. Monica stayed inside. She locked all the doors then wrapped her arms around herself. Turkey went around to the passenger side and tapped on the window with his knuckles.

"Hey, lady, please open the door. We need to talk to you," he said.

"No!" she said. "Go away."

"Leave her alone," Ronald said. "She hasn't done anything wrong."

Joe slammed Ronald in the chest with his palm and pressed him against the Galaxie. Ronald had gone almost ten years without fighting and now he was about to get punched for the second time in less than forty-eight hours. This punching would hurt.

"She did something wrong when she got involved with you," Joe said. "And you did something wrong when you screwed with Lamont. Now you're going to pay the price."

"Lamont's a dirtbag. Why are you standing up for him?"

"Lamont's a good man, not a sneaky reporter like you. Lamont helps people. He's got more character than a hundred reporters. He gave Turkey a job when he got out of prison, and he helped me get hired by the police when Hawk fired me. What do you do to help the world? You write lies. You sneak around. You get people to tell you secrets. You're always calling police liars. You're always trying to get people kicked out of office."

Joe Stoneman became unhinged.

"You're always writing about these pollution things or a congressman taking bribes or some dumbass atrocity in Vietnam. Did you know girls wouldn't even talk to me when I came back from Nam because they thought I was a baby killer? Do you know how many hours I've talked to psychologists at the VA? You don't care, do you?"

Ronald had never written those stories. This wasn't just revenge for taking down Lamont. Joe and Turkey saw Ronald as a proxy for Watergate and the Vietnam war and every television story that told them something was wrong with America. It was a dangerous case of guilt by association.

"I just write cop briefs for *The Eagle*," Ronald said.

"We're not going to hurt this woman, but we are going to hurt you," Joe said. "We want to make sure she knows what a chickenshit you are. We want to make sure she understands she needs to keep her mouth shut." To Turkey he said, "Get her out."

Turkey lifted his leg and kicked the passenger window with the heel of his right boot. Monica screamed. Turkey reached through the window frame and opened the door, then pulled Monica out of the car. He pulled her upright and grabbed both her arms.

"You're hurting me," Monica said. She was breathless and looked like a child compared to Turkey.

Ronald headbutted Joe. The big cop stumbled backward. Freed, Ronald ran around the car and faced Monica and Turkey. He was no match for Turkey, but he had to try. He rushed Turkey and threw a running punch with his right hand. It glanced off Turkey's face.

"Oh boy," Turkey said.

He tossed Monica to the ground like a used tissue. Joe came from behind and grabbed Ronald's arms and pinned them with a double chicken wing. He lifted Ronald's feet off the ground three inches. Turkey stepped up, his eyes shining and his lips wet with saliva. He was turned on. His biceps stretched the sleeves of his white T-shirt. Monica got to her feet and ran into a pasture.

"You come into my town and act so high and mighty, like you've never been drunk and driving a car before," Turkey said. He slapped Ronald's face with one quick stroke. "Like you never fuck up. Like you're better than me. That's bullshit." He slapped him again.

"I'm just doing my job," Ronald said. "I'm just telling people about bad stuff that shouldn't be happening."

"You don't care about bad stuff. You just care about you. You're just trying to make a name for yourself so you can get the hell out of Millerton."

Turkey had figured him out. He'd summed up Ronald's ambition in a few quick sentences. Ronald had learned a lot about himself in parking lots.

Turkey widened his stance for a better punching angle. Ronald kicked him in the balls. It was a direct hit. Turkey bent over on the side of the road moaning and cursing Ronald. Joe Stoneman released Ronald and spun him around. He pounded Ronald in the stomach with his right fist. Ronald fell toward the ground, but Stoneman grabbed him and slung his body against the side of the Galaxie. Ronald couldn't breathe. Stoneman's knuckles crunched into the left side of his face. He tasted blood. At least Monica got away.

Joe Stoneman didn't throw more punches. He heard the sirens. He saw the blue lights as two patrol cars braked beside the Galaxie. The cops silenced the sirens but left the lights pulsing.

"Hey, guys, this joker was giving me some trouble but it's under control," Joe called out. "Thanks for the assist. I'm about to book him. Resisting arrest—the usual stuff."

Dwight Bennett, wearing the khaki uniform of the Miller County Sheriff's Department, stepped into Ronald's field of vision.

"Take your hands off the reporter," Dwight said. "You've already done enough damage. You're outside your jurisdiction."

"Dwight," Ronald said.

"Dwight," Joe said, keeping his grip on Ronald's shirt collar. "It's good to see you, brother. We need you to keep these scumbags under control. When did Hawk hire you?"

"I said unhand the reporter. Put your hands on this car." Dwight placed his palm on his service revolver. "Turkey, put your hands on the hood of the Galaxie."

"What the hell," Turkey said. "This jackass attacked me. I'm not the criminal here."

Chief Deputy Sammy Nichols stepped into the light and pushed Turkey toward the car. "Move it," Nichols said. Two other sheriff's department cars arrived. Two deputies got out. The Stonemans were outnumbered.

"We've been keeping an eye on Ronald," Nichols said. "Hawk's orders. We expected something like this would happen. Dwight volunteered to help on his first day on the job."

"Come on," Joe said. "This guy is a reporter. I'm a cop, and I'm just doing my job. Whose side are you on?"

Nichols replied, "You have the right to remain silent ..."

CHAPTER FORTY-ONE

When Ronald pulled into Monica's driveway the next morning, her green Corolla wasn't there. He knocked on the door and Monica's mother answered in a tennis skirt, looking lean and healthy.

"Oh God, Ronald," she said, seeing the purple bruise covering his face. "Are you okay? And your car?"

He'd covered the passenger window with a flattened cardboard box attached with duct tape. It was something a real Millertonian would do.

"I'm fine," he said, though talking hurt his jaw. "I wanted to make sure Monica was okay. Is she here?" He already knew the answer but wanted to go step-by-step in the discovery process.

Mrs. Timbes put her hand on Ronald's shoulder. "She wasn't hurt. She's not here. She packed her car and went back to Florida this morning."

Hearing it hurt more than knowing it.

"She didn't stick around to find out if I was all right?" he said. "I could have been killed defending her from those big guys."

"After those men attacked her, Monica had to walk through the country for a mile before she found a house. The people let her use their phone and her dad drove out and picked her up. Her dad called the sheriff's department and Hawk gave him a full report. He said you were banged up but survived. Monica felt like it would be for the best if she hit the road. She asked me to give you this."

She withdrew an envelope from her tennis dress pocket. No return address. Mrs. Timbes gave him a quick hug and shut the front door with a soft, clicking finality. He read the letter in the driveway while sitting in his car.

"I'm sorry I didn't say goodbye, but I had to get out of Millerton as soon as possible," Monica wrote. "Things have reached a crisis point in my life—not just with you and me, but with my entire existence, my academic future, and my relationship with my parents."

For somebody at a crisis point, her handwriting was perfect—a smooth, flowing cursive that would have been a pleasure to read under other circumstances.

"When Barry filed for divorce, I thought it would be like terminating a legal contract with a business partner, but I was wrong. Marriage is a big thing, even a marriage with problems. I tried to pretend that it didn't bother me, but I couldn't concentrate on my studies. I couldn't sleep, and I started eating hamburgers and unhealthy foods. I came home to sort things out, but I couldn't make up my mind about what to do. Then I met you. You're so different from Barry. You don't over-intellectualize things. The time we spent together will always be precious to me."

Ronald couldn't believe she wrote that line. When he said something like that to her, she accused him of lifting words from a cornball movie. He couldn't call her on it because she was already in another state.

"You helped me make up my mind about what to do, even if it was by accident. When that big man manhandled me like a rag doll, I was terrified. The terror jolted me into deciding to make changes. I'm going back to Gainesville and finalize the divorce with Barry. I want to finish my doctorate. I need the life of the mind that can only be found in an academic setting. Life in Millerton, and life with you, was too rough for me. I'll never forget you. With affection, Monica."

Monica had beaten him to the breakup punch. He drove into town, pulled into Burdette's Superette, and parked on the shady side of the building. He reread the letter. Monica was a coward for not telling him goodbye to his face, but she was right about one thing: marriage was a big deal. That's why he was upset when Barry walked into the house. Making a relationship legal meant you were serious.

CHAPTER
FORTY-TWO

Ronald was bruised and sore but would not be denied the satisfaction of writing about the Stoneman brothers' arrest. Ronald was part of the story, so recusing himself would be the ethical thing to do, but nobody else in the office could write cop news like him. If you had to choose between good ethics and a good story, the story won.

At the sheriff's department, a deputy escorted Ronald back to Hawk's office. Hawk sat behind his desk clipping his fingernails.

"How you doing?" Hawk mumbled, not looking up. He was wearing a tie clasp of crossed pistols.

"Fine, considering what I went through last night. I came close to being killed."

Hawk grunted. He clipped the pinkie nail on his left hand.

"I wanted to say thanks for having Sammy Nichols watching out for me," Ronald said. "And thanks for hiring Dwight Bennett. That was a good move. The sheriff's department saved me from a big-time beatdown. I'm going to write a story about what happened. I need a statement from you and I need to know what charges the sheriff's department will be filing against Joe and Turkey Stoneman. They haven't bonded out of jail, have they?"

Hawk used the edge of his hand to collect the clippings and slid them off his desktop into his cupped left palm. He shook the clippings into a round trash can, laid both palms flat on top of his desk, and looked at Ronald.

"I didn't hire Dwight Bennett to make you happy. I did that because we had an opening, and I needed a qualified officer. Secondly, Chief Deputy Nichols and I had a long discussion about that incident with Joe and Turkey Stoneman. After conferring with the district attorney's office, we have decided it would be in the best interest of the people of Miller County if no criminal prosecution occurred."

Ronald held his ballpoint pen in his right hand. He held the notepad in his left hand. He had nothing to write.

"No charges? Are you kidding? Look at the bruise on my face. Joe Stoneman knocked the living crap out of me. Turkey slapped me and kicked out a window in my car. They dragged Monica out of the car and tossed her around. Are you going to let them brutalize an innocent woman? Are you going to let two violent sociopaths walk free?"

"Sociopaths? I didn't know you were a psychologist."

The corners of Hawk's mouth twitched upward. The office door opened. Sammy Nichols eased into the room and took a chair against the wall.

"It's always a judgment call when we decide to make an arrest," Hawk said. "We weigh a whole lot of factors. In this case, there's no written report as far as I know. Your girlfriend decided to leave town without making a statement. I know her parents—we've been friends for a long time. They said they'd rather not have her name dragged into this, and I've decided to honor their wishes. You got roughed up a bit last night and I'm sorry about that, but nobody got killed. We had to decide what's best for the overall community. That's why we're not filing charges. Right, Sammy?"

"That's right, Sheriff," Sammy said. Ronald had never seen the man smile before.

"I don't get it," Ronald said to Hawk. "You know that Joe Stoneman is a threat to public safety."

"I think you're exaggerating things. We don't prosecute every infraction that passes before our eyes," Hawk said. "We exercise discretion. I'm sure you've gotten away with doing something illegal since you've been in Miller County, like driving down our country roads while smoking marijuana."

This was a different side of Hawk. Not friendly, not politicking. He was threatening Ronald and doing it with a happy face.

"Are you ready to meet that guy?" Hawk asked Nichols. They stood and walked out of the office. Two more people who didn't bother saying goodbye to Ronald.

At the police station, Ronald waited at the front desk while Betty Stokes talked to a man who said his neighbor shot at his dog because it pooped in the neighbor's yard. The dog wasn't wounded, just scared, and Betty promised to have an officer come out and talk with the neighbor.

When the man left, Betty said, "Nice shiner, Scoop."

"What happened?"

Betty opened her hands wide. "Justice has been done."

"I think you and I have different definitions of justice."

"Joe Stoneman resigned from the police department, and he'll be moving out of town before the end of the week. Turkey's moving with him. You can rest easy because you won't see them around."

"This is unbelievable. What's going on? Hawk wouldn't tell me."

Betty motioned for Ronald to lean in. She whispered, "Hawk and Chief Smithers ate breakfast this morning at Melton's Restaurant and hashed things out. They figured it would be bad for Miller County law enforcement if it became known there was a rogue cop beating up a hard-working reporter and his girlfriend. Especially since the cop had worked for both the police department and the sheriff. They came up with this compromise. The Stonemans leave town and nobody goes to jail. Problem solved."

She looked at Ronald with the same self-satisfied half-smile that Hawk had. The cop smirk. It said, we've done something you don't like but you can't stop us.

"I'm going to write a story. This is collusion. The people need to know."

"What will you base your story on? You didn't get an incident report from the sheriff's department. Your editor likes documents, remember? And if you do write a story, what's the point? The bad guys are out of sight and out of mind. As far as you getting smacked in the face—people would say that's an occupational hazard for stirring things up. Nobody would care. That story would be a flop just like your story about Lamont wrecking in Jorgensen's yard."

She'd complimented him on Lamontgate the day it was published. Now she belittled his story. Betty shifted with the wind. He turned for the door.

"It's not always about you, Scoop," Betty called out. "It never was."

CHAPTER
FORTY-THREE

Bill Jorgensen stood on the sidewalk in front of *The Eagle* building, looking out of place. Ronald had left his life in shambles. Ronald had tailed Jorgensen around town like he was a child molester on the loose, invaded the privacy of his desk in the equipment shed, read his poetry without permission, outed him as a secret poet, and stood witness when Sarah lashed him with ridicule. Ronald had set fire to Jorgensen's marriage—that sacred bond between a man and a woman that Ronald now understood was of the highest importance. When Ronald walked up, Jorgensen extended his thin, pale hand and said, "Thanks." No mention of Ronald's bruised face.

"Thanks for what?"

"For writing the story about *My Life in Limbo*. I was wondering when the photo's going to be shot. Also, could I look at the story before it's printed, so I can make sure everything is accurate?"

How could somebody so old, so homely, and so unemployable be so self-obsessed? Ronald hadn't written the story about Jorgensen's book and never intended to. He'd been stringing Jorgensen along until he could nail him for feeding at the public trough. But Jorgensen didn't see Ronald's manipulations. Ronald resolved to make things right with the man, who was collateral damage in the war against Lamont Moody. He'd write the story. He'd talk Martha into letting it run.

"I'll schedule the photo right away and we'll sit down for another interview."

"When will it run? I want to buy a hundred copies of that paper."

"I'll let you know in advance, and I'll slip you some free copies."

Jorgensen sighed with relief. "What are you doing now?" he asked.

"I thought I was going to be writing the defining story of my newspaper career, but it fell through. So, nothing much."

"Want to get high?"

They walked around the corner to Jorgensen's car. Jorgensen moved legal pads off the Vega's passenger seat and tossed them into the back. They sputtered down Main Street, drawing disdainful looks from pedestrians. Jorgensen turned down Water Plant Road and pulled a joint from his pocket. They rolled up their windows for the joint lighting, then rolled them down once it was burning. Ronald turned the radio dial but got nothing.

"It works about half the time," Jorgensen said.

How could he ride around in a car, stoned, without music? Ronald forgave Jorgensen because the pot was good. Trees whizzed by. A kid standing in his front yard waved. It was a beautiful day.

"Where'd you get this dope?" Ronald said.

"A friend mails it to me from overseas, and I pick it up from my postal box, just like Sarah accused me of doing."

Ronald had hoped her name wouldn't come up. "Sorry about wrecking your marriage. I crossed a line."

"We've had problems from the beginning," Jorgensen said. "When we met, we were both hurting. Her husband had just died, and my wife split for Texas with that guy. Sarah valued me at the beginning, but she wouldn't stop talking about money. Ever. That's what drove us apart. After she kicked me out, I went back to the house, and we had a fight like you wouldn't believe. I said things I'd been holding in for years. It was cathartic—an emotional orgasm. We're getting divorced! And she wants it to happen so bad she's going to pay for it with her bedpan money." He chortled. "Thanks for destroying my marriage. I couldn't have done it without you."

Jorgensen smacked the dashboard with the heel of his hand. Magically, music spilled out of the speaker.

EPILOGUE

SIX MONTHS LATER

The going-away party started at Bob's Fish House, where Snap consumed fifty-two fried shrimp to defeat Ronald in the eating contest. Next, the group went to Exiles to hear the John Johnson Blues Band, except somebody stole John Johnson's red Fender guitar out of the van an hour before the show. He could only play with that guitar, none other, so the band broke down the equipment and went home.

"Thank God," Snap said. "They're terrible and they don't even know it."

"You're certainly critical of your fellow musicians," Ronald said. "What about your band, Blue Smoke?"

"I'm looking for a new drummer. Frederick's girlfriend said he had to quit or else she'd break up with him. He sold his drums and cut his hair and he's going to church on Sunday. Wimp."

Frederick's girlfriend was gorgeous. Snap's band was going nowhere. It was the right decision, but Ronald would never say that out loud. Snap needed his fantasy of a musical future.

Marcus and his girlfriend, Marie, walked in and joined them at the table. From their smiles, Ronald surmised they'd just gotten stoned *and* had sex. Shelly arrived with a tray of beers balanced on her fingertips like an experienced waitress.

"To the ones who got away—Ronald and Marcus," Shelly said, raising her plastic cup. "Congratulations on moving up in the world."

"Thanks, Shelly," Marcus said. "You've helped me so much along the way. You've given me so much great advice."

Shelly leaned over and kissed his cheek. "Our loss is *The Washington Post*'s gain."

"Quit moving in on my boyfriend," Marie said. "Right in front of me?"

Marie was normally not one to banter, but Marcus's success emboldened her. His photo of Shelly punching Lamont had been picked up by the Associated Press. It ran in papers across the country. After Marcus returned to college, the picture won first place in the North Carolina Press Association contest for spot news photography among daily papers with less than 10,000 circulation. He applied for—and won—a summer internship in *The Washington Post* photo department.

"Way to go, Marcus," Ronald said. Marcus owed most of his success to Ronald. Ronald not only told him to get the camera that night at The Food Mart but also tackled Andy the cop to prevent the confiscation of the camera. Ronald put his physical safety on the line for the First Amendment. Did Marcus ever say thank you?

"I'll say hello to Bernstein for you. Woodward, too," Marcus said.

The table went quiet as Linda Lasseter walked up and stood at attention. Nobody thought of inviting her because of her moral opposition to alcohol.

"Somebody would like to speak with you," she said to Ronald. She pivoted and walked away.

In the parking lot, Ronald found Linda standing beside Dwight. They were a legitimate couple now and talking about marriage. As a sheriff's deputy, Dwight was prohibited from entering Exiles.

"I wanted to talk before you moved," Dwight said and stuck out his hand. "Congrats on the new gig. It's a big move up from Millerton."

The Winston-Salem Guardian had hired Ronald to cover the news in nearby Glendale County. He got the job after winning first place in the press awards in feature writing. The story was about "The Mill Town Poet Laureate." His lead: "Bill Jorgensen says he's a simple craftsman, no different from the men and women working grueling shifts at Millerton's furniture and textile factories. But instead of creating sturdy tables or tightly woven blankets, Jorgensen manufactures something timeless: Vivid and vivacious verse."

The wire services picked up the story. Jorgensen sold more books of poetry and with his newfound fame, was hired as a guest instructor at his old school, Elon College.

It helped Ronald that Martha had put in a good word with her old colleagues at *The Guardian*. They welcomed Ronald as if his hiring was predetermined. He would earn an extra twenty dollars a week and was given a title: Glendale County Bureau Chief. It was a one-person bureau.

Ronald and Dwight talked about old times like they'd played on the same sports team in high school. Being polite didn't feel like the moral compromise it used to. Ronald had come to realize that he'd be dealing with guys like Dwight as long as he covered the cops, so he might as well get used to it. Every police agency in the world was populated with ballsy bullies who might, under the right circumstances, save your life. It helped that the army records arrived and showed that Dwight had, in fact, seen combat in Vietnam.

"You know, you changed my life," Dwight said. "Without you, Linda and me wouldn't have gotten together. Too bad about Monica. I thought you two made a good couple."

How did he come to that opinion? Had he been spying on them the whole time? Had he been working with Joe Stoneman?

"It never would have worked out with Monica and me. We were too different. She belongs on a college campus, and I belong here, in the real world." He started to explain the rise and fall of the relationship but remembered he was talking to Dwight, who would use the information against him sooner or later. "I'm playing the field now. I've even had a few dates with a fellow journalist, Dawn Mourning from Channel 5."

Dawn said she might come by for the celebration, but she was just being polite. They'd only had two dates and she wasn't the type to set foot in Exiles. She did like to drink beer, though.

"You really are moving up," Dwight said. Ronald and Linda executed an awkward goodbye hug. Ronald watched them drive away in Dwight's Cutlass.

He stood in the parking lot. Grains of glass sparkled on the asphalt under the light of the utility pole. Tractor trailers whooshed down the Millerton bypass. The bar door opened and three seconds of Lynyrd Skynyrd escaped into the sky. He waited to hear a train whistle in the distance. It didn't happen, so he went back inside, wishing Monica were there to complain that Exiles didn't serve white wine.

THE END

ACKNOWLEDGMENTS

Thanks to Reagan Rothe and the staff at Black Rose Writing for turning my idea into a book. Thank you, Paolo Aguila, for a great cover design. Ron Aiken, Charlene Ball, Barbara Brockway, Deborah Geering, Susan Percy, Victoria Phillips, Chris Rapalje, Mary Stokes, and Libby Ware are friends and critique group members who provided invaluable feedback in the creation of this novel. Thanks to Janie Mills for her editing expertise and good judgment and George Weinstein of the Atlanta Writers Club for creating a community of writers. Konstantin Toropin advised me on military records from the Vietnam era. Julia Ellis, my daughter, gave me valuable advice throughout. My wife, Susan Puckett, is my first editor. She cheered me on during the writing process. I will be eternally grateful to the late Wint Capel, who took a chance and gave me my first newspaper job. Most of all, I want to thank the hundreds of reporters and editors I've worked with in the news business over the decades. You inspire me.

ABOUT THE AUTHOR

Ralph Ellis is a journalist who has worked for small-town papers, big-city dailies, and digital news organizations. He has three adult children and lives in Decatur, Georgia, with his wife, food writer Susan Puckett. He is a graduate of the University of North Carolina and pulls for the Tar Heels. His website can be found at ralphellisauthor.com.

NOTE FROM RALPH ELLIS

Word-of-mouth is crucial for any author to succeed. If you enjoyed *The Accident Report*, please leave a review online—anywhere you are able. Even if it's just a sentence or two. It would make all the difference and would be very much appreciated.

Thanks!
Ralph Ellis

We hope you enjoyed reading this title from:

www.blackrosewriting.com

Subscribe to our mailing list – *The Rosevine* – and receive **FREE** books, daily deals, and stay current with news about upcoming releases and our hottest authors.
Scan the QR code below to sign up.

Already a subscriber? Please accept a sincere thank you for being a fan of Black Rose Writing authors.

View other Black Rose Writing titles at www.blackrosewriting.com/books and use promo code **PRINT** to receive a **20% discount** when purchasing.